Frederick William Robinson

In bad hands and other tales

Frederick William Robinson

In bad hands and other tales

ISBN/EAN: 9783337137281

Printed in Europe, USA, Canada, Australia, Japan

Cover: Foto ©Andreas Hilbeck / pixelio.de

More available books at **www.hansebooks.com**

IN BAD HANDS

AND

OTHER TALES.

VOL. II.

IN BAD HANDS

AND

OTHER TALES

BY

F. W. ROBINSON

AUTHOR OF

"GRANDMOTHER'S MONEY," "NO CHURCH,"
"THE COURTING OF MARY SMITH,"

ETC., ETC.

IN THREE VOLUMES.

VOL. II.

LONDON:

H URST AND BLACKETT, LIMITED,

13, GREAT MARLBOROUGH STREET.

1887.

CONTENTS

OF

THE SECOND VOLUME.

THE LUCK OF LUKE SHANDS.

(CONTINUED.)

THE LUCK OF LUKE SHANDS.

CHAPTER II.

'THE QUARRELLING OF LOVERS IS,' ETC., ETC.

LUKE SHANDS was a very fine specimen of
Felspar manhood, and manhood ran there to six
feet one, as a rule. Luke had run over. He
was six feet two, with a chest like a bull's, and
hands like sledge-hammers. Why a man with
such latent force in him should have been for
twenty-five years of his life such an unlucky
fellow—a sober, hard-working young herdsman
as he was, too—is not to be accounted for any
more than why he should be so particularly good-
tempered over it. He was always laughing,
even at his own bad luck; he would have his

B 2

jest, and be none the worse for it. That he had
never been able to save money enough to marry
Peggy Brantwell was the only thing he had not
roared with laughter at; but there were odd
little points of humour. about that even which
made him smile, if with a little effort at times,
like a twinge in the wrong place. And there
he was laughing at Peggy's surprise and fright
and discomfiture, as at a huge joke which really
was worth a little extra hilarity that evening.

'Did you see me come out?' she asked,
quickly.

'Yes, of course I did.'

'Then it's all spoiled, and I've had my trouble
for nothing; and you ought to be ashamed of
yourself for following me about in this way,'
cried Peggy. 'I—I shall never forgive you,
Luke,' she added, whimpering, ' never.'

'I'm sorry I've put you out, lass,' said Luke,
becoming suddenly grave, 'and, of course, I
didn't mean it—but what have you been a-say-
ing of to the lady? Now come—a clean breast
of it. Won't you?'

'How did you know I was up here?'

'Cock-eyed Dobson,' he explained. as they proceeded down the winding path together, 'told me he'd seen you go by, and I thought you had gone to Mother Twitters, who's down with flemsy, and wheezes awful. And then I caught sight of Tom Crasp, sneaking and dodging about the bushes, and I followed him. And I scared *him* a bit,' said Luke, with a sudden and prodigious roar of laughter, which scared Peggy in her turn, and made her slip a step or two ; 'and *he* went home in a hurry. Hadn't you better take hold of my hand ?'

'I don't want your hand.'

' You're not as sure-footed as usual, lass. It was Tom,' he continued, 'who told me you'd gone up to yon chapel.'

' Tom's a sneak. I'll never give him a halfpenny again.'

' He's not worth it.'

' And I'll never forgive you,' she added, ' spying and prying after me like this, just as if— just as if—you thought I was—I was not to be trusted by myself, for a moment. It's not fair. It's not like you.'

'No; it's not like me,' asserted Luke, 'and it's not like you, lass, to come a-clambering up here and saying in the cave all sorts of gibberish that a pack of silly women have been a-talking to you about. Mother Twitters for one, I'll be bound. I know her.'

'Never mind,' said Peggy, startled by Luke's proximity to the truth, and taking refuge in a phrase that committed her to nothing, and at the same time asserted that spirit of independence which he had aroused.

'It's not as if you haven't been sensibly brought up,' said Luke, gravely, ' or were one of those wenches in the village. It's just the sort o' thing I can't abide in man or woman, Peggy; hardly in a child. I can't abide it.'

'Then don't abide it,' said Peggy, pertly; 'that doesn't matter to anybody, I suppose.'

'I should hope it would matter to you,' he said tenderly, now, 'and if it don't matter what I say or think, why, you're not my Peggy, but some other lass who's come out of My Lady's Chapel instead of yourself.'

'You shouldn't make me angry.'

' You shouldn't have gone up there all alone, Peg,' he said, reproachfully; ' there's some rough fellows at the quarries about, and it's late and dark. And you might have fallen, and it's a steep way down too. Catch hold of my hand —do.'

'No, thank you, Mr. Shands.'

Luke Shands looked gravely at her, and then said :

' I shouldn't have thought it of Peggy Brant-well, if anybody had told me but herself, that she could go off in a tiff and temper because the man who likes her was afraid she might come to harm. I couldn't have believed it.'

' It isn't as—as if——'

And then Peggy, meeting a sob on its way upwards, made a gurgling noise, and swallowed it to disguise her emotion.

' And blest if I believe it even now,' he added.

' I—I didn't want to be seen.'

' Just as my luck has turned, too—just as a little streak of good luck seemed coming to you and me—that you should go on like this,' he said.

' What!'

'And snap me up just like that old grandfather of yours. I wish,' he cried, a little crossly himself, · that I may never be lucky again, if this is to be the end of it.'

' Oh! you wicked——'

And then Peggy burst into tears, and frightened Luke, who drew her more closely to his side, and soothed and caressed her, and was very nearly crying too. Thus the storm ended, and the sheet lightning flickered away, and before the lovers had reached the village they were laughing and talking together, and the best of friends.

'And what is the good luck, Luke?' she asked, as he did not speak of it again, indeed—such is the aggravating habit of the male sex in general —seemed to carefully avoid a subject upon which he knew she would be anxious. ' Why don't you tell me?'

· Well—Uncle Ribton's dead.'

· Oh!' exclaimed Peggy, 'how dreadful! And you call that luck?'

' Well—Uncle Ribton never saw any of us

for years—he wasn't unlike your grandfather, I've heard, not but what *he's* very pleasant at times if he likes. I've no cause to fret much because Uncle Ribton's dead. I don't even re-member what he was like when he was living, you see.'

'That makes a difference,' said Peggy, thoughtfully.

' And, as he has no relations so near as I am, the lawyer wrote to me to-night to say I've come in for his pigs.'

' His what ?'

' His pigs. He was a pig-dealer in Neltes-combe. Haven't you heard me say so ?'

'Did you get that letter by this afternoon's post?'

' Yes.'

' Just at sundown ? That was when I was praying for good luck to you, Luke.'

'Were you, though ? Well, that's a little strange, ain't it,' said Luke, 'and for me too. Bless you, Peggy, let me kiss you for that before we go any further.'

That little ceremony having been gone through satisfactorily, Peggy said :

'It doesn't seem to matter anyone seeing me go in or out of the "Chapel"—I'm so glad.'

'Perhaps something'll happen to spoil it,' said Luke, with another long laugh, 'as it has not been done according to Mother Twitters—it *was* Mother Twitters that put all that nonsense into your head, wasn't it, now?'

'Well, Mrs. Twitters did mention it,' Peggy confessed.

'Your grandfather said long ago she was a witch, and ought to be drowned.'

'Poor thing! And how many pigs are there, Luke?' asked Peggy, returning to the main subject; for upon those pigs hung the destiny of this young couple.

'Five; and one of 'em's blind,' replied Luke.

'Oh, good gracious, all this fuss about five pigs!'

'It's a stroke of luck,' said Luke Shands again.

CHAPTER III.

A SUNDAY BARGAIN.

LUKE lived all alone in a tumble-down, one-roomed shanty, close to the hills of Felspar. He was worse housed than even Felspar folk were housed as a rule. The Irish mud huts were roomy and capacious in comparison with many of the domiciles where the villagers of this remote district drew the breath of life.

It was a cottage perched by itself some ten feet below the level of the narrow path in front of it, so that a spiteful person passing by could have easily kicked the roof off, and it possessed a back garden of some twenty feet in length, ending abruptly with the white, blank hill-side, a colossal wall of four hundred feet which

towered above it and shut out air and light.
In the distance, from the valley and the lower
ground, Luke Shands' cottage seemed growing
out of the jagged limestone like a wen, but there
was room in the garden behind for the pigs, if
those animals would not object to a little over-
crowding.

And Luke had brought his pigs home, and
Matthew Brantwell, a shrewd business man in
his old age, toddled over to see them, and to
see too what could be done. Whether Luke
could not be 'done' might be added, even without reflecting too severely on the character of
Matthew, who was certainly an unreasonable
and covetous old gentleman. Everybody knew
that—even Luke, who thought the best of most
people, Mrs. Twitters excepted, had his suspicions of it, though he made a great deal of
allowance for the eccentricities of Peggy's
grandfather.

For Peggy's sake, and at Peggy's wish even,
Luke was always extra civil to Matthew Brant-
well, a civility which was not often reciprocated,
Matthew's temper being a bad one. For

Peggy's sake even he was living in this cottage, as a tenant of Mr. Brantwell's, at four pounds per annum, a sum of money for which Luke might have secured quite a comfortable room at Cock-eyed Dobson's, and without the bother of housekeeping. But Matthew had persuaded Luke two years ago to take the establishment after his mother's decease, and Luke had thought it as well to please the old gentleman, not caring much where he lived until he settled down for good with Peggy. It was only to sleep in ; all day he was in the valley, or on the hills with the sheep, and in the early evening he was courting Peggy—Sunday excepted, when he and she walked seven miles to church in the afternoon, with three or four other devout inhabitants of Felspar, the rest of them stopping at home from year's end to year's end.

It was on Sunday morning that Matthew called on Luke, who was shaving by a bit of glass hung up in the front window, which Matthew banged at with his walking-stick and cracked.

'I've come to see the pigs,' said Matthew,

who was an authority on pigs. 'Peggy tells me you've had quite a bit of legacy.'

'Yes, Master Matthew, I call it luck myself.'

'Your Uncle Ribton and I have done many a stroke of business together, Luke,' said the old man; 'and if he had lived twenty-four hours longer I should have had those pigs, and there'd been a matter of—well, ten pounds, very likely, in his stocking instead.'

'Oh!' said Luke, as he put away his shaving tackle, 'I've heard they're worth a lot more than ten pounds. But I ain't a judge of pigs.'

'They're very ugly.'

'They're uncommon ugly,' asserted Luke, 'but they're very healthy.'

'They'll eat you out of house and home.'

'Yes—they do eat,' said Luke, with a sigh, 'but there's a chance of getting their own living down the valley. I let them out every day.'

'You'll lose 'em.'

'Oh, they know their way back to supper,' said Luke, with one of his laughs, 'trust them.

But they're so aggravating, I wish they wouldn't come back sometimes.'

'Why don't you sell 'em, then? You're not able to keep 'em in ease and comfort, as a pig should be kept, any more than you have ever been able to keep yourself—though I say it as shouldn't, p'raps—in ease and comfort. But I'm a plain-speaking man.'

'You are, sir.'

'Why don't you sell the pigs, then?'

'Bless your heart, I'm going to,' said Luke.

'Eh—what? What's that you say?'

'I'm going to sell them, and bank the money, before the winter comes on. At least, I'm going to sell four of 'em.'

'Well—well then, what do you want for the four?' asked Matthew. 'That's what I've come all this beastly way for—and my legs so bad too—to ask if I should take 'em off your hands. The five, I mean—I want the lot. What's the use of keeping one pig?'

'I shall stick to the blind one,' said Luke, very firmly.

'Why?'

'Well, my old mother was blind the last two years of her life, and the pig reminds me of her very much.'

Matthew Brantwell sneered at this touch of sentiment, but he said no more about the blind pig just then.

'Let's look at them,' he said, shortly.

They passed into the little space behind the house, where were the five animals, all with their noses turned towards the gate which shut them out of the valley. Luke was right—they were uncommonly ugly. A misshapen, rhinoceros kind of pig, four of them red-eyed, as though they had been crying, and the fifth with his eyes bunged up for ever.

The sight of them excited the cupidity of Matthew Brantwell.

'I'll give you twenty pounds for the lot. Say it's a bargain, and don't be a fool, Luke,' he said.

'I can't drive a bargain on a Sunday, Master Brantwell,' answered Luke; 'not that I'm a religious man, hard and fast as I ought to be— but I promised Peggy I never would again.'

'Peggy's always got some nonsense in her head, and a-interfering about something.'

'Peggy's always right, only she's a bit superstitious. Nothing ever came right that was done on a Sunday, I've heard her say over and over again, bless her.'

'Never mind about Peggy. We're talking about pigs, ain't we?'

'I'd rather not talk about them any more till Chipstoke comes to see them.'

'Chipstoke—what, from Roundell Pikes?' exclaimed Matthew.

'That's the man.'

'What do you want to see him for?'

'I don't know that I want to see him,' replied Luke. 'He sent me word last night he wanted to see me. That's all. Except that he said, "Don't part with the pigs till I've made you a good bid."'

'Selfish beast,' said Matthew, 'that's like him —I know him of old—and then he'll offer you less than I have. See if he doesn't. He'll want them for a mere song, and you'll be sorry presently you didn't let me have them.'

'I don't say I won't sell them to you. You're Peggy's grandfather.'

'To be sure I am—Peggy's grandfather, exactly so.'

'And you shall have them for what he offers me—there.'

'Oh!'

Matthew Brantwell seemed checkmated for a moment. What might not Chipstoke offer if 'dead-set' on these pigs, and knowing what pigs they were? And what might not Chipstoke make of them, being an expert in pigs—a specialist—a pig-collector?

'Luke, if you don't let me have these pigs now, I'll forbid you ever coming to my house again,' he spluttered forth. 'I'll move out of Felspar, and take Peggy with me. I'll go and live in London; I'll be shut of you altogether.'

'Good Lor'!' exclaimed Luke, in horror.

'I hate Chipstoke—and he mustn't stand afore me.'

'Of course not,' said Luke. 'I never said he should.'

'Look here, Luke Shands. I'll tell you what

I'll do. I'll give you this cottage—this freehold property—for them. There, you're rent-free for life—needn't' worry about rent any more—can save up, and build another little room here presently, so that when you marry Peggy——'

'When—I marry Peggy!' cried Luke. 'Yes, yes, go on.'

'Well, it will come to that some day, I daresay,' said the old man. 'At all events, when you marry somebody, you can take her to a good roomy place, as this would be, and say here's our home—rent-free—now and for ever. And you may keep the blind pig—there.'

'Done!' cried Luke.

'Done!' echoed Mr. Brantwell,

The two men shook hands, and clenched the contract.

'We'd better not say anything about this to Peggy till it's all settled,' said Luke, after a little reflection; 'as it *is* a Sunday bargain, after all.'

'Certainly not. Not a word to Peggy.'

'Shall I give you a bit of writing about it?'

'Yes; and date it Saturday, Luke. It looks so much better, too.'

It is astonishing how quickly that bargain was concluded, and how the freehold of Luke's cottage was made over to Luke by a lawyer who came from Neltescombe on purpose, and how Luke became his own landlord, and felt very proud of the new position he had secured. But when he met Peggy the day after the four pigs had gone home, leaving their blind companion in Mr. Shands' possession, a little light —even a strong, lurid light—was thrown upon the whole transaction.

'Luke, do you know what you have done?' she cried, with tears in her pretty blue eyes, 'and done without telling me anything about it, of course?'

'Done? Yes; got a house of my own over my head, at last.'

'You great big silly, what's the good of such a place as this? You might have bought it for less than fifty pounds at any time, and you've let him have four pigs.'

'Well?'

'And they're exhibition pigs—prize things, and worth forty pounds apiece. And grandfather has sold them already, and is laughing at you.'

'Your grandfather is a sharp old man, and I'm a dull young ass,' said Luke, looking very grave.

And that was all he had to say at Matthew Brantwell's 'besting' him.

'I knew something would happen to you for watching me at "My Lady's Chapel,"' said Peggy. 'I knew what it would come to. I wonder where it will end now.'

'I wonder what that blind one's worth?' said Luke.

CHAPTER IV.

THE LUCK TURNS IN GOOD EARNEST.

THE blind pig was not worth much—indeed,
was not of the same 'strain,' and was not even
fit for pork when the winter set in in real
earnest, and the animal caught cold, and went
blundering about the back yard, coughing like
an old man, or leaning against the rock at the
end of the garden, too weak to get round the
premises without taking a good rest by the way.
The pig suffered very much from cold, and
Luke, being a good-tempered and feeling fellow,
took the animal indoors for one night on the
Hibernian system, when it had a shivering fit
that nearly brought the house down, and

screamed so loudly to get out again, that Felspar thought there was murder doing somewhere in the valley, and ran for the one policeman of the place—who had gone ten miles over the hills to a supper-party, and could not be brought back to duty under six good hours.

'That pig's going to die, Peggy,' said Luke, when he saw her again. 'Did you ask your grandfather whether he'd make a bid for him?'

'Yes, and he said he wouldn't have it at any price.'

'He's very ill,' he said. 'Do you know what I'm going to do?'

'No,' said Peggy, a little alarmed, for Luke was *not* particularly wise when the impulse seized him.

'I've got some dynamite charges from the quarry, and I'm going to blow him a sty out of the rock—a good, big hole, where he can get in out of the snow and the wind, poor beggar.'

'Oh, you must not do that.'

'Why not? It's my rock. It's part of the freehold,' he said, with a laugh not quite so hearty as usual.

'Yes, it's your rock, but you'll blow the freehold down, Luke.'

'Ah! I had forgotten that.'

'The house was condemned months and
months ago, only grandfather kept it to himself.
And the surveyor says it'll have to be rebuilt,
or he won't answer for the consequences.
That's why grandfather wanted to sell it in a
hurry.'

'Yes; I know. I've had notice instead of your
grandfather,' said Luke, ruefully. 'Your statement's quite correct, lass.'

'And what's to be done?'

'I don't quite see. I shall have to chuck up
the freehold, I expect.'

But the next day the blind pig was so very
ill, and the mist came swooping in such bitter
gusts down the valley, that Luke Shands resolved to carry out his original intention.

'It will bring the house down, too, I daresay
—and I don't care if it does,' he added, 'the
darned old lucifer-box that it is. Yes, I'll chance
it.'

So Luke Shands, in a desperate kind of mood,

full of anger against his house, and of sympathy
for his pig, laid his plans and his dynamite, and
went to work in a business kind of way, having
done good service in the quarries at times, off
and on, for a change. Hence he lighted his fuse,
and retired a little way down the valley, leading
his quadruped at the end of a string, and there
waited the result with grave composure. But
Luke's luck kept pace with him. The report
came, and the crash of cliff wall followed, and
the pig died of fright there and then—turned
over on his side and gave up the ghost forth-
with.

‘ That's a settler,’ said Luke ; then he marched back, and found his house standing, with only
the roof blown a trifle askew, and looking as if
it had got a cocked hat on. And the hole he
had blown into the cliff was black and cavern-
ous, and seemingly without end—and, what was
the most remarkable part of the whole occur-
rence, it had all gone inwards, as though the
charge had shattered a thin crust of limestone,
and driven a way into the heart of the
hills.

'Bless and save us, this is a queer start,' said Luke Shands.

It was a queerer start than Luke imagined, than Felspar had imagined, than scientific folk had imagined, until they came down presently in twos and threes, and accounted for it clearly and graphically, and said it was just what might have been expected. Luke had not expected anything, and it was not till he had lighted a candle and passed into the hole that he discovered he had blown a passage into a cavern, long and tortuous and seemingly winding its way now up and now down to an extent that, on the spur of the moment, he thought he would pursue no further.

'Why, here's a lady's chapel all to myself in my back garden,' he said, with one of his hearty roars, and then he was startled by the rays of his candle-light falling on what looked like a lace curtain with tints and traceries from roof to floor.

'That's very queer,' said Luke.

But the first scientist who came to see this—

and he was handy on the spot, and had been foraging about Felspar with a hammer for the last week—said:

'That's one of the grandest stalactites I have ever seen in my life.'

And the cavern was full of stalactites and stalagmites of all shapes, sizes, and colours, when one came to explore it carefully.

'You'll exhibit this,' said one of the wise men. 'Have the gas laid on, and charge so much a head.'

'Can't afford it,' said Luke.

'Oh, but you'll have plenty of people here presently. I shall write an account in the " Universal Geological Chronicle." Is this your own property?'

'Yes, sir.'

'You're a lucky fellow. Do you know the man who owns the cavern in the Crockaway Hills?'

'I've heard of him.'

'He's worth twenty thousand pounds.'

Luke sat down on his garden palings and felt as if he should faint away on the spot.

'You don't say so!' he said.

'But I do.'

'You'll excuse me, sir, but I must run and tell Peggy.'

And away Luke started down the valley at a pace that might be set down as headlong, and Professor Treguffin seized the opportunity to chop off one small stalagmite that he was sure would not be missed, and which would add considerably to the character and tone of his own private collection.

There is not much more to be told. Shands' cavern was soon famous in the Felspar district, had its place in guide-books, became a feature of interest in the locality, and was lighted up by gas presently, having a little gasometer all to itself, on the site where the blind pig died. And all at Luke Shands' expense, when Luke began to get a rich man, and that with some degree of rapidity. The last Easter Monday before Matthew Brantwell died, three thousand excursionists came to Felspar valley from the new station a mile and a half away, and most of them paid a shilling apiece admittance without a murmur. After that Matthew Brantwell died of jaundice, and was buried with his fore-fathers.

Luke and his wife—need I say, Luke's wife was Peggy Brantwell, whose grandfather had cut her off with a shilling?—and the children are living in a brand-new stone house at the head of the valley where the Felspar hotel is now.

It was in this strange fashion—and true fashion—that Luke Shands' luck turned, and in her heart of hearts Peggy still puts it down to her little prayers in My Lady's Chapel that autumn evening when the spell seemed broken by her lover's untimely interference. But Luke will not have this; and Mrs. Twitters—who is still living, we rejoice to say—thinks that a man who could have had such luck as he had, and not be grateful to it, and own how it came round to him, is little better than a born heathen, and does not deserve to prosper.

JACOB AND POLLY.

JACOB AND POLLY.

JACOB CATTLEY was a messenger to Messrs. Perkinson, Goldchest, and Co., the rich bankers in Lombard Street. At least he always considered himself attached to the establishment as a messenger, though he had never 'signed articles' with the principals, and was just tolerated outside on the pavement, at an acute angle of the building and three feet from the street-doors, where customers and clerks were not likely to tumble over him. He had been hanging outside this big bank for many years now, and it had become a custom of late days to send him on little errands which were not within the pro-

vince of a regular clerk's duty, and which the
clerks of Perkinson, Goldchest, and Co. would
have scorned to perform at any price whatever.
If anybody required a cab, Jacob was sent for
one; if a country gentleman with a big balance
on the books wanted to be shown the way to
the Bank of England, or Billingsgate, or the
Tower, Jacob was told off as guide; if something was wanted surreptitiously by the clerks,
n the shape of a newspaper or a ham sandwich,
Jacob was sent for it, and there had been times
when it was even considered safe to trust him
with a telegram.

Jacob received no salary, but was supported
by voluntary contributions, like a hospital, and
what those contributions amounted to in a year
there had been much speculation concerning, at
the bank, amongst the clerks.   It was set down
by young and imaginative minds, as a 'pretty
penny, take it altogether!'   But taking Jacob
Cattley altogether was, to the ordinary observer,
to set him down as a poor, half-starved, ill-clad,
miserable old man, struggling hard to live, and
always on the brink of failing at it.   A shabbier

old gentleman was not to be found between the Bank and Houndsditch; but he was never in rags, and he always boasted a clean face under his rusty-brown top hat, which he poised at the extreme back of his grey head. He did not appear to flourish on his contributions, but grew thinner and more pinched with every week of his outdoor service there. 'You can see him shrivelling away,' one young man had seriously asserted. 'He's a regular miser, I'll be bound.' And with his hollow cheeks, and peaked nose, and prominent chin ground fine to match that poor pinched nose of his, he might have been taken for a miser, or a pauper, or indeed anything deplorable.

Still he had what the clerks called his 'tips,' and Mr. Goldchest, every Saturday morning, when he left the bank, and before he stepped into his carriage, the door of which Mr. Cattley always opened for him, gave him something, it was noticed, but whether a sovereign or a threepenny-piece was a matter of uncertainty, the claw-like hand of Jacob closing so quickly on the gift. The junior clerks thought it would

be a 'threepenny,' Mr. Goldchest not being a
liberal paymaster, in their humble opinion, for-
cibly expressed each quarter-day, but Jacob,
probably of a reticent disposition, never let
them know, and, at all events, he did not wax
fat on his emoluments; and in the rainy and
frosty seasons caught many a cold and cough,
and wore, winter and summer, the same suit of
grey threadbare clothes, to which, in very in-
clement weather, a red cotton neckerchief,
relieved by white lozenges and tied in a strange
knot, was added, by way of protection, to a
giraffe-like throat.

Jacob was considered a poor hanger-on; but
Jacob had his hangers-on too, and people whom
in his turn he took upon himself to patronise.
There are always depths below depths in this
eccentric world of ours, and always some poor
brother and sister to whom a hand can be held
out, or a little kindness rendered, and Jacob
Cattley had his dependent in the background,
and one who waited and watched for him as
regularly after banking hours on Saturdays as
he waited and watched for Mr. Goldchest about

noon; and this dependent on Mr. Cattley was
a dark-haired, dark-eyed purveyor of penny
'button-holes' and twopenny bouquets, a poor
flower-girl who regarded Mr. Cattley as a
regular customer on Saturdays, one who was
always good for a penny, sometimes even two-
pence, when he had been extra fortunate in the
City.

Jacob, it may be said, never purchased his
flowers in Lombard Street; no one in that busy
centre had seen Jacob Cattley spend a penny-
piece upon anything, but once away from the
City proper, and hurrying on towards Blackfriars Bridge—on the Surrey side of which he
lived, and which he crossed regularly twice a
day to and from his 'place of business,'—anyone who had taken the trouble to watch him—
which no one ever had—would have seen Jacob
somewhere in the neighbourhood of Ludgate
Hill bargaining with Polly Baxter for a nosegay
every Saturday afternoon.

Jacob Cattley would even condescend to
patronise Polly Baxter, and to occasionally pass
a remark upon the weather, or the extent of her

stock-in-trade ; but all this was done in an aus-
tere, stand-offish way, which did not encourage
conversation in return, and which was a washed-
out copy of the great Goldchest manner, when
the big banker skated across the pavement to
his carriage. Polly Baxter did not know this,
and thought it was very kind of the old gentleman in the queer-looking comforter to say a
word or two to her now and then—words
which, with all their coldness, had a little ring
in them of interest or sympathy, or something
not easy to comprehend, and which the flower-
girl did not attempt in any way to account for.
Sometimes she wondered why he purchased
flowers, or what he did with them after he got
home ; he was so particular about the bunch he
purchased, and had so strong a fancy for the
brightest colours.

Suddenly Jacob Cattley was missed from
Lombard Street, and from the neighbourhood
of Ludgate Hill ; and Polly Baxter's basket
blushed with flowers in vain for him. Every
day Polly Baxter had been accustomed to see
him between four and five trotting homewards,

with his sharp face set due south; every day he said 'Good morning,' in a grave, fatherly way, and with a solemn bend of his long neck; and on Saturdays, as we have intimated, he always stopped to bargain with her for her gayest pennyworth. And now Jacob was missing, and no one knew where Jacob lived, so that the mystery of his disappearance might have been solved by a friendly call.

'He's dead, for sixpence, poor old cove,' said one of the junior clerks, a pert and slangy and over-dressed youth, whom Jacob had in his heart disliked, despite the offering of a penny now and then. 'He's off, depend upon it. I'm sorry I was so deuced hard on him last week.'

Polly Baxter wondered more about him than the rest of the community aware of his existence. She did not know why she should 'bother about the old man,' but she did. He was a something removed from her life, a regular customer gone, and that was to be regretted when regular customers were scarce. When she had bought her flowers at Covent Garden Market in the early morning, and had taken them to her little

attic where she made up her penny bunches for
the day, she caught herself thinking of the funny
little bloke, and of his grave, old-fashioned
ways. She had had a father like him once in
some respects, and he had died in the workhouse,
praying that she might ' keep good,' which she
had. Polly was a poor ignorant girl enough,
who had never been taught to read and write,
and her father had been ' a bad lot,' as it was
termed, and had not cared to see her taught, or
cared much about anything save himself, until
he had become a martyr to rheumatism, and lost
his situation in the Market, and had to go finally
into the house, leaving his daughter with all the
world to herself, and nobody in it to look after
her, except a policeman or two, who hauled her
up at times before aldermanic Solons for ' ob-
structing the thoroughfare,' and got her fined
and ' cautioned.' Then the father was sorry,
and woke up to some little thought of his girl,
when he could do little else but think.

Nevertheless, Polly Baxter earned her own
living honestly, and made the best of her
position by thrift and industry, coming very

close to starvation once or twice in the hard
times which will turn up to the hard-workers.
Still she fought on, and had begun to teach
herself to read and write of late days, and to
find her way on Sundays to a little chapel down
a back street, and listen with much surprise to
what they told her there, and to wonder why it
had been kept from her all these years, and why
no one in the highways and byways of her life
had said a word about it.

Possibly thinking of this had made her think
of other folk as the light filtered a little through
the darkness of Polly Baxter's life, but she *did*
think a great deal of the poor old-fashioned little
man who seemed to have vanished like a ghost,
and it became a matter of speculation why he
had ever bought flowers of her at all, being a
man who probably had not much to spend on
the minor luxuries of life. And so regular a
customer, too, thought Polly, with a sigh again.

Suddenly however, the regular customer,
turned up again one Saturday, six weeks or two
months after everybody thought he was dead.
It was like a ghost rising up in Lombard Street,

and even Mr. Goldchest, taken unawares by this re-appearance at his carriage-door, gasped out, ' Bless my soul !' and slipped one foot off the kerbstone into the gutter in his first surprise.

He was even a little curious for so great a man, and said,

' Have you been ill, Jacob ?'

He did not know his other name. ' Old Jacob' was Mr. Cattley's cognomen in Lombard Street ; ' Cranky Jacob' sometimes.

' No, sir.'

' Then——'

Jacob's rugged face twitched very much as he touched his hat deferentially, and said,

' I've had a loss, Mr. Goldchest.'

' Oh, indeed.'

Mr. Goldchest did not ask what or whom he had lost; he glanced at the big rusty hatband wrapped round the rusty hat of his humble dependent ; there was a fugitive fear even that there might be something ' catching' from Mr. Cattley's close proximity, and he stepped with alacrity into his carriage, and drew up his window sharply. He did not reward Jacob on

that occasion; he gave no thought to the arrears
which might have accumulated during Jacob's
absence from his duties, and the old man walked
home very thoughtfully, and with a downcast
expression of countenance. On his way home
he encountered Polly Baxter, who also was disposed to take him for a ghost, and nearly
dropped her basket into the London mud at the
first sight of him.

'Why, lor', sir, who'd have thought of it?'
she exclaimed.

'Thought of what?' he asked, a little curiously.

'Of your being alive and moving about like
this agin. I'm so glad.'

'Glad, are you? What are you glad for?' he
inquired, sharply.

'Glad to see an old customer,' was the truth-
ful reply.

'Ah! just so,' said Jacob.

'And not that exactly, mind you,' added
Polly, 'but because you are here, you know.
That's it. Where *have* you been, sir? Laid
up?'

This was Mr. Goldchest's inquiry also, but not
conveyed with so much interest.   And his
answer was the same as before.

'I've had a loss.'

'Not—not money?'

'I've lost my daughter; all I had in the
world to me; all I cared for, child.   Good day,'
he said, with an excitement for which Polly was
wholly unprepared.

'Yes; but here, *hold hard*, old un,' she cried,
inelegantly; 'ain't you a-going to have any
flowers to——'

The 'old un' hurried away from her, darted
across the road under horses' heads and omni-
bus wheels with almost the alacrity of youth,
and it was not until he was upon Blackfriars
Bridge that he had recovered his composure,
and quite finished with a ragged pocket-handkerchief, which was evidently a segment of his
winter wrapper, being of the same striking pattern and colour.   When he had crossed the
bridge and Southwark Street, and was turning
into one of the little crowded thoroughfares on
the left of the Blackfriars Road, leading to the

salubrious quarters of Gravel Lane and parts adjacent, he was astonished and discomfited again to find Polly Baxter at his elbow, exceedingly red in the face, and short of breath.

'Well, you jest can stump out, guv'nor, and no flies,' she said.

'What do you want with me?' he asked, testily now; 'what—what is it? How dare you?'

'I only want to say I'm sorry like,' she blurted forth. 'I didn't think, all at once, about the flowers, and that you wanted them for *her*, of course, who's gone now, and who was fond of flowers. I twig, I see; you won't mind what I said—will you now?'

Jacob Cattley stared at her, but he croaked forth, very hoarsely,

'No.'

'I'll never ax you agin—I'll never look your way agin; but take this, please, for this once, won't you?'

And Polly held out his usual-sized bunch of flowers, at which the old man shrank back, as though it had been a pistol levelled at him.

'It isn't for the money,' said Polly, excited now herself; 'I don't want any money—ketch 'old, please do. Jest to make believe you're taking them to her the same as ever, sir.'

The old man stretched out a trembling hand towards the flowers at this suggestion, and Polly thrust them into his grasp, and fairly ran away across the bridge again, leaving him looking after her open-mouthed, and with some salt tears brimming over his blinking eyelids and making their way down the deep furrows in his cheeks.

On the Monday, Jacob passed her as usual on his homeward route, and with his old, patronizing bow, and with a steadier stare at her too, as if no longer afraid to face her. But Polly looked the other way, and would not see him—fell into the habit of hiding from him even—and on the following Saturday would also have eluded him, had he not come up the reverse way of the street, and taken her unawares by a flank movement.

'Let me have a good bunch to-day—a two-penny bunch,' he said, in quite a business-like manner.

Polly Baxter was surprised, but she gave him the flowers he required, and he dropped the money into her basket.

'But you don't want 'em now—do you?' she murmured.

'Yes, of course I do. That was a good thought of yours, child, last week. *And I took the flowers to her.*'

'Oh!' ejaculated Polly.

'And shall do so every week, making believe, as you say, that's she waiting for them. It's not a bad thought at all,' he muttered; 'she was so very fond of flowers.'

'How old was your gal?' asked Polly.

'About your age, I should say.'

'And ailing allers, was she?'

'For the last three or four years, yes. Good day;' and then Jacob hurried away, and this time she did not attempt to follow him.

It was from this time that Jacob contrived to be as regular a customer to Polly Baxter as he had ever been, and had anyone had the curiosity to follow the movements of the old man, he or she would have seen him every Sunday, in fair

weather or foul, plodding on to Tooting cemetery, to lay his little offering on the grave of the
daughter who had been always fond of flowers.
When the winter time came on, and flowers grew
very scarce and dear, and Polly was compelled
to raise her prices, the old man looked very pale
and pinched with cold, and did not move along
with his customary alacrity—on the contrary,
limped painfully at times with the rheumatism
which had seized him.

One very cold Saturday she said to him,
suddenly :

' You ain't well ?'

' Well, not quite as well as I might be,
perhaps,' he answered, cautiously.

' I don't mind your paying for these some
other time, you know,' she added, hurriedly,
' if——'

' If what ?' he asked, as she came to a full
stop.

' If you're hard up. It won't make much
difference to me, and *she* might miss 'em now.'

' Thankee,' he said, gently; and he looked
very hard at her from under his tangled, wiry

eyebrows; 'that's a kind thought, child. What did you say your name was?'

'I didn't say,' she answered, surprised in her turn; 'but it's Polly Baxter.'

'Living where, now?'

'St. James's Row,' she answered, 'at the back there. But why?'

'Good day.'

That was the last time Polly Baxter met Jacob Cattley in the London streets, for Jacob disappeared again, and Lombard Street and the flower-girl on Ludgate Hill missed him altogether.

'He must be dead this time, poor old cove!' thought Polly.

But Polly was again deceived. One morning, a short, red-faced woman, with a market-basket on her arm, and a key in her hand, looked hard at her, and stopped.

'Is your name Baxter?'

'Yes.'

'Polly Baxter?'

'Yes, that's it.'

'You're wanted in George Street, Gravel

Lane, No. 29. My lodger, the old man who used to buy flowers of you, wants to see you precious bad.'

'He ain't dead, then,' cried Polly; ' well, I *am* glad.'

' Don't see what you're got to be glad about,' said the old woman, sharply; 'but, no, he ain't dead yet. He's hooking it off, though, sharp enuf.'

' Oh!—is he ? Oh ! I hope he ain't!'

' Can you find your way?'

' Yes. Trust me for that.'

Polly Baxter trudged away at once to George Street, and to No. 29, where, on the top-floor, she found poor Jacob Cattley, very much down in the world, and with very little life left in him. The rheumatics had got an iron grip of him at last, and fever had followed, and this was very nearly the last of him, as the red-faced woman had prophesied.

As Polly entered the room, he smiled at her as at an old friend.

'Polly,' he said, speaking with great difficulty, ' I wish to put you in mind of an old offer to me.'

' What's that, sir ?'

' I want you to open a credit account with me.'

· A what ?' cried Polly.

' It's a term we have in Lombard Street,' he explained, quite airily, 'to trust me, I mean, for a little while for a few flowers.'

' To be sure I will !' cried Polly. ' Right you are.'

' I'll pay you soon ; and I want you to do more than that, much more.'

Polly waited and wondered till he took time to recover his breath ; then he added,

' I want you on Sunday afternoon to take them to *her*, and lay them on her grave for me. Do you mind very much ?'

' Not at all,' said Polly. ' I'll go direkly after chapel, if you'll tell me how to find it.'

' Do *you* go to chapel ?'

' Yes, reg'lar.'

' Good girl. Keep that up.'

' No fear, sir.'

' And come and tell me regularly what they tell *you* there ; will you, child ? I should like to know.'

'To be sure I will, sir.'

'When you come back from *her*.'

Then he gave his directions which Polly Baxter carried out faithfully, until the end came, and Jacob Cattley was buried with his daughter.

After his death, Polly Baxter went regularly to the cemetery just the same, and laid her little bunch of flowers on the grave of him who had said kind words to her in life. That was the end of him, and of the story, she thought, until one day, a week or two afterwards, a prim little gentleman in black called upon her, and asked her many questions and made perfectly sure that she was the genuine and only Polly Baxter, flower vendor, before he surprised her with his news.

Jacob Cattley had been a bit of a miser, after all, and had scraped together, by his faithful and humble services in Lombard Street, the sum of one hundred and fifty pounds. He had died without a relation in the world to care for him, and he had left his money to Polly Baxter, of 49, St. James's Row, City, E.C., in remembrance of her kindness, and 'in settlement of his credit account with her.'

Polly Baxter is married now, and she and her husband have a flourishing little greengrocer's shop and are doing very well. There are fresh flowers on the old man's grave at Tooting, and one grateful heart keeps his memory green.

.

DICK WATSON'S DAUGHTER.

DICK WATSON'S DAUGHTER.

YES, sir, Portland born and bred, and proud of it. We Portlanders are a bit proud of it, a good many of us, this being always home to us, as it has been to our fathers and mothers before us, don't you see? Can't say exactly why this should be always home—it's not easy to explain, and I am not a good hand at explanation. Has anybody ever explained why cats love houses and back yards and not the people in them? why they will starve on the tiles, or in an empty house rather than go with the master who has fed them all their lives? Something to do with the overgrowth of the organ of locality a wise-

acre told me once, and perhaps he was right.
But old dad said he was a fool, and dad was
just as likely to be right as the other man. I
don't always know a fool from a wise man
myself; it takes a lot of time to find out that
even in London, where you are all so mighty
sharp.

I stick to Portland. Do you see Weymouth
and Melcombe over yonder in the bay? I've
never been across, and shall never care to.
What's the use? I've everything I want—
health and strength; a good house, and a good
wife; plenty of work, and plenty of smiles to
meet a man after the work's done. What more
should I find over yonder?—and how much less?
My father lived and died here, so shall I. I
can't abide with people always wanting change
—that's a bad complaint, sir, you take my word
for it, and gets people into all sorts of trouble—
into prison too, poor gommocks. I'd lay a
crown-piece there's a lot of them up at our big
prison there, who could say to me, ' That's true
enough, David Costerbadie, if you never speak
another sensible word in the whole course of

your blessed life ; that's uncommon true.' Very
well then, what's there to laugh about ?   I daresay your London is a fairer, squarer place than
this, but it would not suit me any better for that.
Not it.

Well, *perhaps* a few years ago I was not
quite as satisfied as I am now, and was bother-
ed just a little with an idea of sliding off, of
turning out a soldier, or a policeman, or a diver
—which my uncle was, and got drowned by
way of a judgment on him, the dad has always
said, for sneaking away and getting under
water.   But, though it did cross my mind I had
better make one less, it never came to the big
march to go, and matters worked round by
degrees, as they will, sir, if you only wait and
work hard and don't snivel.   Bless you, yes !
It won't come round the way you thought—
dashed if it ever does that !—but round it comes,
just like the hand of a clock, and as I'll prove
to you clear enough if you don't mind listening
for a while.   Mine's a queer story in its way.
When those young ones about us grow up, I'm
a-going to tell it them, even with their mother

sitting by to hear it. I don't know there's much
of a moral in it, but Betsy says there is; and
Betsy has always her wits about her, if I haven't,
though she's not Portland born and bred, as we
Costerbadies are. She's a foreigner, she is—
ain't you, Betsy lass?—and very much ashamed
of it too, though it wasn't her fault, poor thing,
as some people might think. She comes from
your town—from a part of it called Whitechapel
which sounds like a place clean and pious
enough for anybody, and Betsy says perhaps it
may be in the parts of it she doesn't recollect.

It was her coming to Portland which made
all the fuss about us, and put us all to sixes and
sevens, as the saying is, although we were at
sixes and sevens before she turned up, for that
matter, owing to hard luck. There had been
bad times at the quarries—the private quarries
were all wrong somehow—changing hands and
changing men, and the new stone they fetched
out of the land did not come up well, or did not
last long, or had something or other the matter
with it which kept us quarrymen chopping
and changing, or sitting still in the house-place

out of work, and wondering when the work would come again. We grumbled a bit, too, at the prison lot taking the labour from our hands, and letting us lie idle. But people *will* grumble, and Government wants its quarries worked at a cheap rate; and at all events here the prison is, for good or bad, and no getting rid of it again. We're a bit grown to it, and, with work enough for both of us, we don't grumble as we used.

Betsy Watson crossed over to Portland in the bad times then, when work was very slack, a score or more of years ago I may say, before the railway came to us, and the big breakwater was finished. I mind her standing in the street with a big bundle in her arms—a crimson bundle with white spots—and looking round as if she'd lost her way, and a poor, thin, pale, gawky kind of wench she was that day. Just to think of that, sir, looking at her now, that wide!

She came over by the steamer, and, when the people had all got on shore and gone away, she walked slowly along the road towards Chesil—

that's the lot of old houses by the Chesil bank, which we see from this window down on the shore there. We all lived at Chesil at that time, a family of us Costerbadies, dad and mother, and sister Leah, and young Jonathan, who was a cripple and died before his time, and your humble servant. I had been out of work all the winter, and was hanging about the road as if I had stolen something—and ready, if anybody had asked me, to carry anything up town or top of the island for a stray sixpence or less. And there was nobody I could be of use to but Betsy Watson, who strolled on with her black straw bonnet blown to the back of her head, and who was wondering where she was, or which was the right way to go, or what had become of those who should have been at the landing-stage to meet her and help her with her bundle, and say, ‘How d'ye do?’ and had not come to time, or never meant. It was something of this, I fancied, before I caught her eye and slouched away a step or two, and then stopped again with my mouth all open like a trap, Betsy told me afterwards, and looking a rare silly.

It was she who spoke first—women being naturally more forward in their ways than men, or being more inclined to settle things off-hand, and not to go beating about the bush so much as we shy fellows. And I was shy enough of strangers, of course, though this bit of a gawky girl was ten years younger, and like a child to me. She was exactly seventeen, and I was seven-and-twenty. She was five feet seven, which is a strapping height for a girl, even if she has overgrown herself a bit, and I was six feet three ; so there you have us like a picture, and a rum picture we must have been too.

' Do you know, sir, where I could find a cheap lodging in these parts?' she asked, bang off, of me.

' Oh ! there's plenty of lodgings,' I answered, pointing to no end of bills in all the windows of all the little and big houses in sight. It was Easter time, when company was scarce enough, and the weather was awful cold that year. It was actually snowing while she spoke to me, and the snow was settling on her hair like flour on a bright brown chestnut.

'Ye—es, but I want a very cheap lodging. I don't mind how poor, being poor myself,' she added, frank and straight.

'Oh! I see.'

'And I shall not give anybody any trouble while I stay here ; that is, I hope I shan't.'

This was a very young woman to come out holiday-making by herself, and, indeed, for all her height, I took her to be a year younger than she was, she was that thin, and had so innocent a face. A sad face, too, and sorrowful people do not look younger than they are, as a rule ; but she did somehow.

'The sort of lodger people like, lass,' I replied, with a laugh, 'and you'd suit a good many about here.'

I did not speak to her as to a lady born, but as to one of my own class, though I was as red all the time as beetroot. And I was wonderfully taken by her, as by a child that had lost its way and wanted help to find it, and might not get into careful hands, being ignorant of life. She was very poor, although neat as a new pin, and well shod. The wind did not quite seem to suit

with her thin black dress and wisp of a shawl,
though, but to cut through them both, as she
stood there trying not to shiver. I thought of
all the neighbours in Chesil, and along the hill-
side, and, not being quick to come to conclu-
sions, I did nothing else but think and keep my
mouth open. When an idea came to me, I gave
her the benefit of it, but it was not very often,
as we walked slowly along the road together.
I should have been glad to carry her bundle,
but did not like to ask.

'They let lodgings down there,' I said, pointing to Chesil, ' but it would be awful cold for
you, and sometimes the sea swamps you when
the wind keeps in this quarter long. There's
old Drucc's, there's Churchfunnel, there's Mother
Dreak's, there's——'

'David, who's this wench?' said a shrill voice
—my sister Leah's voice—and sure enough
there was sister Leah at my elbow, as curious
as any woman, and wondering who I had got
to talk to and walk with all of a sudden at that
time of day.

Betsy Watson looked at Leah, and crept aside

like a girl a bit frightened at the sight of her.
And Leah was not a well-favoured lass, I must
say, not for thirty-five, when good looks are not
always in their bloom even with good temper
to back them, which Leah never had. Leah
had grown very yellow of late and full of hard
lines, and had lost two front teeth only last
week—one top, one bottom—and that would
make any woman cross, though there was no
one to see her but dad, and me, and mother,
and Jonathan. Leah had been out marketing,
and had come upon us with her basket on her
arm, and a something green sticking out of the
basket. She had no bonnet on, and the wind
was blowing her hair—almost grey now—a
good many ways at once, and her face was
pinched and not so clean as I had seen it now
and then on Sundays. She looked a bit spiteful
at us both, too, goodness knows for why.

'This young girl,' I said to Leah, 'was asking
me where she could get a lodging hereabouts,
and I was saying——'

'Oh! you're a pretty one to talk about lodgings,' Leah answered, uncommon sharp; 'what

kind of lodging do you want?' she asked, with a 'long steady stare at Betsy, and then at the bundle in her arms.

Betsy told her what she had told me, and more. She wanted a very cheap lodging; she was poor; it had been said she must have change of air, and she had saved up all the winter to get that change, and here she was. It was all plain speaking, and no beating about the bush.

'For how long?' asked Leah.

'A fortnight—perhaps three weeks, if my money will last out, and I can get to like this place,' she answered, with a little shudder at it already.

'You came from—where?'

'London.'

'You've come a long way, if you're short of money,' said Leah, with a kind of snort.

'They said this part of England would do me a deal of good, and besides——'

She did not say what besides, but stopped all of a sudden, and my sister, more interested in Betsy's means of living and paying her way

F 2

than in her reason for giving Portland a look-
up, said, bluntly,

'What money have you got?'

'That's not for you to ask, Leah, or for me,'
I broke in here; for I saw the poor, weak thing
flinch again at the question coming from such a
stranger; 'that's no one's business but hers.'

'Yes, it's my business,' said Leah, 'for this
child—and she's but a child, tall as she is—may
not be able to pay those who'd feel the ill-luck
of being cheated of a penny."

'Oh! I don't want to cheat anybody,' said
Betsy Watson, quick and warm at this. 'When
the money is getting low, I shall be ready to
go home.'

'I should think Mother Dreak's would suit
her, because——'

'Because you know nothing about it, David,'
said Leah, 'or about anything save quarry
work, which you can't get. If this child can
pay her way—fair and square, as she will—she
might spend her holiday in a worse fashion than
along with us, I take it.'

'Oh! no,' cried Betsy, shrinking away for the

third time, ' I—I don't want anything like that.'

' How do you know what it's like, or what
we're like ?' said Leah, ready to argue the point
at once, and with no end of force too—just like
Leah, that was. ' We're neat and clean; there's
a bed-room all to yourself, with a fine big sea-
view, too. We'll board and lodge you cheaper
than anyone in Chesil, and we haven't had a
lodger for nine months, and this hulking brother
of mine is always out of work, and you will be
a help to us. One house is as good as another,
if it's an honest house, ain't it ?'

' Ye—es,' said Betsy, frightened from all argument by this; ' oh, yes! quite true.'

' Then what do you want to go anywhere
else for ? Come and see the house—there it is:
it won't kill you to look at it. That's my father
sitting in the doorway—there's my mother looking over his shoulder at us—there's Jonathan at
the window—*your* window. You come and see
the place before you say, " I don't want anything like that;" you mayn't know what you do
want;' and Leah seemed to drag Betsy Watson
down the road to the stone houses in the shadow

of the Chesil bank, where the waves were dash-
ing and roaring finely that afternoon, and with
a noise that skeered her first go-off.

I walked a little distance behind; the way
my sister talked had swept away a little objec-
tion of my own which I should have liked to
make, but I was clean silenced by her style. I
had never known Leah go on quite like that
before, never seen her so excited and so anxious.
Generally Leah was a woman of few words,
which were plain and hard enough when they
did come out, which was not very often. 'A
sulky toad,' I have heard father call her more
than once, and 'A sour lot, that Leah Costerbadie,' had been said of her by the Chesil neighbours for no end of time. Leah had never
seemed particularly anxious about anything till
that day—but then it was hard to guess whether
she was anxious or not. So her manner opened
my eyes as much as it did young Betsy Watson's, just for the reason I was no more used to
it than she was.

When we got home, Leah said to me, ' You
wait here, while I show the young lady over

the place ;' and 'the young lady' looked at me
for a moment as if afraid to trust herself with my
rampagious sister ; then she gave way and passed into our house as if she was Leah's prisoner,
and there was not much chance of running away
from her.

Presently she was talking to father and mother
in the parlour, and Leah slipped out and caught
me by the arm.

'She'll stop if you don't blunder out something, and turn her against us,' she whispered,
hoarsely.

'Yes—but don't you see——'

'You fool!' she cried, 'don't *you* see ever?
Ain't we starving!'

She backed into the cottage again, leaving
me all of a big heap against the stone wall.

It was as bad as that then, and it was harder
lines with the Costerbadies than I had guessed.
Well, the old people, and Leah, and Jonathan
had fought their battles well without my guessing much about it, and without my wondering
how long the money would hold out. No one
had worried me, fretful as they all were in their

way, for I took things about as quietly as most folk, even when there *was* anything to put me out, which was seldom, though Leah and dad had a bad way—I own it—of aggravating people, and each other. Not so much in bad times, for then we held together a bit more, and helped each other all we could. Presently my brother Jonathan—poor cripple and hunchback he was, and yet close on twenty years of age— came limping into the street towards me.

'Davie, she's going to stop,' he said; 'she thinks the place will suit her.'

'Well, I hope she'll like it,' I said, 'and I hope you'll all be kind to her, for she's a poor body enough.'

'Yes, ain't she?' piped Jonathan; 'I wonder what she came for?'

'Change of air.'

'Did she tell you so?'

'Yes.'

'I like her face,' said my brother, after thinking it over a little, 'but it wouldn't be lucky if she died here, would it?'

'Lor' bless the fellow—no.'

'It would be our luck though—wouldn't it ?'

'You shut up, and keep that nonsense to yourself, Johnnie—she ain't a-going to die,' I said; 'what's made you think of such stuff as that ?'

Going to die, indeed ! Why, in twenty-four hours from the time she set foot in Chesil she was a different young creature altogether, and as full of life as ever she could stick ! I don't suppose change of air ever agreed with a young person as it agreed with Betsy Watson ; there was quite a colour on her cheeks next day, and before the week was out she was as brown as any berry.

'That Whitechapel of yourn must have been a very sickly place,' I said to her about the third day of her stay with us, and when she was getting redder and redder, nose and chin especially, 'for you to have got as pale as when I saw you first.'

'I can't say if it's sickly,' she answered, doubtfully, 'all I know is I am very sick of it.'

'Were you born there ?'

'Oh, yes !'

' People don't get sick of where they're born
—at least, we don't in Portland.'

' No.'

' But Whitechapel mayn't be quite as fresh a
place as this, take it altogether.'

'1 don't think it is *quite* as fresh,' she answered, laughing at me.

' Then what makes you stop?'

' Oh ! you're as curious as your sister,' she said
pettishly, and went away from me and sat on
the Chesil bank, and chucked stones into the
water for hours afterwards. I felt she did not
want my company; I walked away till tea was
ready, and thought of what she had said all the
mortal time.

As curious as my sister! Well, Leah was
curious enough, I knew, but I had never been
called curious before, and never had been that I
knew of. ' You don't seem to me, David, to
bustle about quite enough or take enough
interest in things,' the dad had told me over and
over again; ' you're too big and lumpy like !'
And now here was a little chit of a woman telling me I was curious, and running away from

me because I worried her with questions—
actually worried her!

Yes, it was singular, because somehow, sir, I
was curious about her. She looked to be so
very much alone in the world, so adrift like, and
yet a contented little soul, very quick with her
needle, and not too much of a lodger. She
liked to be of help in any way, knowing she was
poor, and fancying herself almost one of the
family after awhile. And she *was* of help, and
Leah, who was never backward in making use
of people, put upon her, as I thought, before
the week was out, and got her to run on errands
and do all kinds of things for her, even to re-
shape and fit her Sunday dress—which Leah
had had for years—in the new tip-top Whitechapel fashion, too, which Betsy knew all about,
of course, being straight from London, where
all the fashions come from.

She was really one of the family by the end
of the week, quite at home, and glad Leah had
not frightened her from it when they had first
met in the open street. They all took to her,
Leah and all, and I do not remember Leah's

taking to anybody before, male or female. Not
that Betsy could see this, not understanding her
so well as we did, and thinking she was always
very cross and snappish, not guessing that if
Leah had not taken to her she would have 'let
her have it,' and screamed and yelled and
jawed at her, as she had done at other people
whom she could not abide, as she had always
done at home when put out by any of us. Leah
was handy at making fishing-nets, and Betsy
Watson, handy at anything, looked on one day,
helped her the next, and at such a rate, too,
that my sister almost smiled.

' You're clever with your fingers,' she said.

' We are in Whitechapel—some of them too
clever,' she added, with a sigh which was not
easy to account for.

' No one can be too clever,' said father.

' Oh! yes, they can,' answered Betsy, briskly;
' too clever by half.'

' How's that?' I said.

' Over-clever people get into trouble, David,'
she answered, thoughtfully now; ' at least, I
have heard they do, Whitechapel way.'

'And that's an affliction, David boy, that'll never happen to you, depend upon it,' said my father, at which everybody laughed, Jonathan the loudest, because it did not take a great deal to amuse him, poor little chap!

How that first week slid away whilst Betsy Watson was amongst us!—though I was out of work, and hated being out of work, 'big and lumpy' as the dad said I was. Though dad did not mean all he said about me, bless your heart! Only his nasty way when anything disagreed with him, or when his cough was bad, and shook all his good qualities into his bad ones. Gracious, but the old man could cough, when put to it! 'Coughs his hardest on purpose,' Leah always said, but that wasn't quite correct; though, when the whole house was shaking, I used to think he did let loose a bit.

The old dad was fond of Betsy, too, in his way; she could not play chequers—draughts, as you may call it—when she first came, but he taught her, and she beat him hollow before the week was up. And mother took to her, and poor Jonathan went over head and ears in love with her—which was silly, to say the least of it, a little helpless cove as he was.

By the end of the week we knew all about Betsy Watson, and what she had not told us herself at starting Leah kept asking her until she did. Betsy worked in a wholesale house Whitechapel way ; 'gentlemen's ties' and that fal-lal rubbish turned out by the ton, and meaning hard work, long hours, and deuce of a little pay for it. The work had taken most of the health and strength away from her before I had first clapped eyes on her. She had no mother—*she* had died when Betsy was a little thing not higher than *that*, sir. And the father? Ah ! here comes the story, and out it came all at once, when Leah was harassing one evening, and I was smoking a short pipe at the open door and listening to every word she said.

Father and mother and Jonathan had all gone to bed, and the two women-folk were sitting up late and working rather hard. I remember it, just as if it was yesterday, and I am likely to remember that night surely.

'Yes, my father *is* alive,' she answered.

'Then why didn't you say so before?' said Leah.

'I didn't think it mattered to you, or anybody else but me,' she said, ay, and with spirit too.

'And what's your father doing, Betsy?' Leah asked.

'He's in David's line.'

'You don't mean that?'

'Up at the prison yonder, working in the quarries, that's where father is,' said Betsy, speaking very quickly now, 'and it's as well you should know it. I don't like keeping anything back; I never did.'

'Bravo, Betsy!' I said, putting my head in at the door to cheer her, and getting my nose snapped off for my pains.

'Isn't it time you went to bed instead of hanging about there at this time of night?' cried Leah. 'What have you got to sit up for? *You* haven't any work to do.'

'That's not my fault.'

'Yes, it is,' said Leah; 'you were never fond of work.'

I should have knocked anybody over who had

told me that outside Portland, but I could not
do anything to Leah, not even shake her. It
was not kind of her, but I said, quietly,

'I can't make work.'

Here Betsy broke in before Leah could say
anything else unpleasant.

'I should like David to know everything as
well as you,' she said, 'because I can trust him
always.'

'Thankee for saying as much, my lass,' I said
back to her; 'yes, you may trust me.'

'My father has been in Portland close upon
seven years,' she began, 'and he has seven years
more to serve, less the time struck off for his
good conduct. A long sentence, isn't it?'

'What's he in for?' asked Leah.

'Housebreaking.'

'It wasn't the first or second time, for him to
get locked up so long,' was Leah's sharp
opinion.

'Oh! no—he has been at it all his life,' said
Betsy, quietly. 'I can't remember ever seeing
my father. When he was not in prison, he was
always keeping out of the way of those who

wanted to put him in it. Once or twice he
called to see me when I was very little—but I
don't recollect.'

' Where were you ?'

' Oh! he paid people to take care of me.'

' Thieves, too, I'll be bound,' said Leah.

'No ; honest people who did not know how
father got his living. That's the odd thing
about my father, and it makes me love him, spite
of everything.'

' What's odd about him ?'

' That he did all he could to keep me out of
harm's way. He had an idea I should never
know anything about him, and that one day
he would turn up a rich man and take me abroad,
to live peacebly there with never a soul the
wiser. Very foolish !' she said, with a sigh,
' and this is how it ended.'

' Just as it ought to end,' was Leah's short
answer; 'I've no liking for a lot of thieves.
And if you have never seen him—how do you
know this ?'

' He writes to me from prison when they allow
him.'

'And he's awfully sorry, of course. That's because they read his letters before they let them go,' said Leah.

'I can't say he's sorry. He never says he is.'

'And when his time is up—he'll thieve again?'

'Yes—very likely.'

'Well, he's a nice brute to love, I must say.'

'He's my father.'

'You'd better have been without one.'

'Don't you love your father, Leah?' she asked.

'Can't say I do particular,' said Leah; 'he's much too aggravating to suit me. But, at all events, he's honest; I couldn't do anything but hate and spit upon a thief!'

'Yes—Leah—I daresay you would,' replied Betsy, 'and I don't ask you to love my father, or to pity him; I know he was very bad—I have read about him in old newspapers, and there was nothing much to be said for him. But still he does not forget me—he writes to me—he is sorry I've no mother to take care of me—and he did the best he could in keeping me away

from him when I was young and he was bad.
You see that?'

'I don't see anything good in him.'

'I do, Betsy,' I said from the doorway; 'at
least, it's my idea he might have made life much
worser for you—and much blacker for you.'

'You get out!' cried my sister; 'your idea
indeed! You never had one in that thick head
of yours that was worth an ounce of sugar.
Who cares for your ideas?'

'I haven't asked anybody to care.'

'Then hold your noise,' said Leah; 'do you
think I'm sitting up to listen to your gabble?'

'Ah, never mind her, David,' cried Betsy at
this moment; 'your sister is kinder than she
cares to let us see, and she doesn't mean all she
says.'

'Much you are likely to know about me,'
answered Leah sharply at this. 'I do mean
what I say—I should be a poor creature if I
didn't. And you, Betsy Watson, might have
told us this before—knowing we are honest
people—and said what you had come for down-

G 2

right. We shouldn't 'a' thought the worse of you for telling us the truth.'

'Here! Lookee here!' I began, when Betsy stopped me by holding up her hand and asking if she had not told the truth,—told more than there was any occasion for, considering what she was and where she was.

'You said you came for your health,' said Leah.

'That's true enough, for I was very ill.'

'And you came for something else besides that. You can't look me in the face, and say you didn't,' went on my sister.

'I am going to tell you what that something else is.'

'I can guess. To see your father?'

'Yes. I have an order from the Directors to see him the next visiting day. That's next Wednesday,' she answered.

'As if I didn't know what you were at Portland for!' said Leah, proud of her cuteness—and she was cute certainly.

'For once in my life,' Betsy went on, 'I thought I would work extra hard to save money to bring me here ; and, in working extra hard, I broke down a little.'

' What do you want to see the wretch for ?'

' What wretch ?'

' Your father.'

' To see what he is like—to ask if I can do any good, or be of any use when he comes out.'

' You'd better let *that* alone,' said Leah.

' It is my duty, I fancy, now.'

' Ah! you're eaten up by fancy,' was my sister's last remark. ' I suppose if he was to be let off you'd go to him, because it was your duty.'

' If he asked me—I would go. Oh! yes.'

' Though you know he's a bad un ?'

' Yes.'

' And that there's no chance to make him a good un ?'

' Still—I'd try.'

' And he'd drag you down instead—that's what it would come to.'

' No ; I should only die. That's all,' said Betsy.

Leah bundled her work together and pitched it in one corner.

'I haven't patience with a bit of a thing like you a-talking like that!' she said, as she walked off to bed. Betsy prepared to follow her, coming first to my side, as I stood smoking outside the door.

'David,' she said, 'have *you* patience with me?'

'O' course I have.'

'Thank you. I am glad of that.'

'So am I.'

'She hasn't,' jerking her little head towards the stairs, up which Leah had tramped without much consideration for those already in bed and fast asleep.

'Oh! you mustn't mind her.'

'She won't have any patience, any mercy— as you will, David, when you are trying to think the best of me, and when you and she know——'

'What?' I asked, as she came to a full stop.

'That I haven't told her everything—that I've kept a good deal back,' she said, all of a flutter now, and not breathing at all regular.

'Have you though?'

'Yes,' she said, in a whisper.

'Well, you're not bound to tell her anything
—or me either,' I said, by way of cheering her
up a peg or two. 'It's not our business.'

'No, it is not. That's where you are right,
David—as you always are—dull as they think
you,' she said.

I was pleased at this. These were kind words
from her to me, and if others thought I was a
fool, she did not, which was comforting. I said
a little more.

'I am only surprised you told her such a lot
about yourself and father, Betsy. I wouldn't
have done it; just as if I'd been drove to it,
too.'

'I *was* drove,' she answered, 'for she knew
already. One of those men with the long coats
and peaky caps was speaking to her yesterday,
and asking who I was.'

'What men?'

'The men who are always about here and on
the hills. The men who walk outside the prison,

night and day, with guns,' she added, with a shiver.

'Oh, the warders! I know.'

'And the men have seen me walking outside the prison, too—for I've been outside, day after day, just as if there was some comfort in being nearer to him.'

'Ah!'

'Do you think he is so very bad,' she asked, 'and quite past hope, David? For it's all truth I have told you about him and me.'

'I daresay there's many worse than the—gentleman. Why not?'

This seemed to console her, for she said after me, 'Why not?' and then walked towards the stairs on tip-toe, stopping with her little foot upon the first one, and looking at me again, so very strangely that I felt curdling and creepy.

'You *will* have patience with me, David. Don't forget,' she said; then she went like a ghost, so quiet-like, to her own room.

She left me a deal to think of, and I was not fond of thinking. I did not like to know she had not told us all, when I came to spell over

the subject, although a little while ago I had
agreed with her. I liked to think her frank,
and with no sham about her. In one week I
had got to fancy her a good deal, and to see her
as different from anybody else as chalk from
cheese. And yet she had been straight-forward
enough for half-a-dozen girls—straight-forward
enough to tell me she was not quite straight-
forward, and to hope I should be patient with
her, when I came to know or guess a little more.
Which was odd—which was more and more
odd, the more and more I thought of it, leaning
against the door-post, with my hands in my
pockets, and the pipe, which had long since
burned itself out, still held tight between my
teeth.

I was very restless that night, and did not
think of sleep. It had been hard to find sleep
since I had been out of work, not having enough
work to knock the wakefulness away from me;
so I leaned against the door-post, and took it
easy-like. For how long I didn't know, but I
must have gone to sleep in the open air, standing up straight, like a statue, or a stuck pig, or

anything you care to call me, sir. It was a
dark night, and warm; the wind had changed
in the last four-and-twenty hours, and brought
a breath of spring with it; I never remembered
going off to sleep in the open air like that before.

The fact was, I thought so much of Betsy, of
all my sister had got her to say, of all she had
said herself after Leah had gone, that I thought
myself silly, and went off clean to sleep. All of
a sudden I woke up with a start, and banged
my head against the door-post—woke up, I
might say, almost in a fright, as somebody
stumbled over my feet, and made a run for it
along the street towards the Chesil bank.

I had got thieves so across my mind, that I
was sure some one had slipped into the parlour
through the open door, whilst I had been dozing, and robbed us Costerbadies, until I recollected as a fact that there was nothing to take
away, and this set me right again. But then,
recollecting—and all this of a flash, though I
was not naturally quick—that the party falling
over me had caught me on the side next the
doorway, and so must have come clean out of

my own house, was to set my long legs after him pretty sharp.

If there was one thing, besides quarry work, that came natural to me, it was running, when I was put to it; and off I went like a rocket after the party, who was scampering along close to the houses, and not going it as fast as a man in a hurry to get away would go, as a rule. When he was in the open, and was running and clambering up the bank, as if he hoped to hide there, or jump into the sea, or something, I could see he had a bundle in his hand, which looked like Leah's bundle, which she had pitched into the corner of the room a little while ago. A sense of being wronged and robbed set me off now at double-quick, and I was on him the next moment, and then over him, and then under him, and then over him again, with my knees upon his chest, and my hands upon his throat.

'Hold hard! Don't choke a fellow! I give up,' the man gasped out; and I was gentler with him, and got my knees, one by one, off his chest.

' Who are you—and what are you ?' I asked.

' Your prisoner—isn't that enough ?'

' No, it isn't.'

' Don't make a row. For mercy's sake, don't make a row until you've heard me out !' he urged; ' I'm clean done for.'

' Is that my bundle ?' I inquired.

' No.'

' You took it out of the house yonder. I'll swear you did.'

' It's my own property.'

' It's a lie,' I said ; ' but get up, you rascal, and come back with me.'

He got up, with a little trouble and some help of mine, and stood by me trembling like a jelly. He was not a strong man ; he saw he was no match for me, and it was not worth his while to try to get away. As he stood up straight, and with no end of trouble too, as if I had hurt him, I saw what he was at once, dark as it was, and with only a blurred outline of a man to look at. I had seen so many poor devils like him—all of one pattern, and not to be wrapped away even by the dark night.

' You've escaped from the prison.'

'Yes, that's it,' he answered.

'How on earth did you manage that?' I asked. 'It isn't often a man gets away from there.'

'And it's hard when he does,' answered the man, sulkily, 'and after all his plotting, planning, working, cursing, praying, to come to such an end as this. I'd rather you shoot me than give me up to them again.'

'I never said I was going to give you up.'

'You're not!' he said; 'good fellow, brave fellow, God bless you, whoever you are! God bless you, sir!'

And the man's voice broke, and his hands, which were shaking like a leaf, seized mine, and wrung them with a tighter grip than when he had clutched me on the beach.

'And I never said I was going to let you go,' I added; at which the man shuddered, and dropped my hands, and slunk back from me. 'It all depends upon that bundle. So just you come back with me into the light. D'ye hear?'

'It's mine, I tell you.'

'Are you coming back, or shall I make you?' I asked.

'I'll come. I can't do anything else. Let me lean upon your arm, if you don't mind, mate. I'm hurt—awfully.'

'Did I do it?'

'No; I scrambled down the rocks from the prison, and missed my footing and fell. So I got up a maimed, damned wretch like this.'

'That's why I bested you so easily?'

'Yes—that's it.'

The man passed his arm through mine, and crawled with me towards the house, groaning with every step he took. We went into the parlour together, where he dropped into my father's Windsor-chair, into which I guided him. I stood over him whilst I struck a lucifer and lighted the candle, which the draught, or the man, had blown out whilst I was dozing at my post. And then I saw, clutched in his hand, a bundle of things tied up in a big red-cotton handkerchief, all red with white spots, the very bundle which Betsy Watson had carried from the steamer on the day she came to Portland.

'Well—you are a thundering thief to begin again so quick—and an awful liar, too!' I said;

'that bundle belongs to this house, and you sneaked it off, a quarter-of-an-hour ago.'

' I said it was my own—and that's the truth,' muttered the man, between his teeth.

' No.   It can't be the truth.'

' And I can't explain.   Don't ask me—what's the use?   Give me some water, for I'm fit to die.'

There was a jug of water on the table, and I held it to his lips, which had turned very grey. Yes, the man was ill, and had been knocked about a good deal, and was fit for nothing, save to pity, perhaps.

I did not know why I should pity him,—but he looked so helpless and broken-down a wretch, with his two big eyes, like an animal's, watching me in fear, and trying to guess by my broad face what I was thinking of. *His* was the face of a man of forty-five—though I thought it was an old man's face as I looked at it then; it was so full of lines, the skin was so dark and withered, and the close-cut hair upon his head was as white as snow. There was blood upon his forehead and nose, and upon his

hands and convict dress—he was a nasty sight
to look at, take him altogether, and it did not
come to my dull wits who he was, and why he
had walked into my house on his way from
gaol. , I was not quick at guess-work ever. I
have said so. It did not come to me till, with
my ears pricked up, I heard the softest tread
upon the stairs, and some one coming down
them, step by step, pausing at each and listening to our talk, and then coming on again.
There was only one who could tread as light as
that in Chesil, and before she joined us I
guessed the truth of it, as I ought to have done
before. I put my hand on his shoulder, and
said, in a low voice,

'Your name is Watson?'

'Well,' he answered, 'and if it is?'

'The father of the girl who's coming to us
now?' I asked, hoarsely.

'Yes,' he said, with a groan; 'God help us
both—that's it!'

It was no use denying it, and he knew it as
well as I did. I daresay he would have told a
lie if he could have done it easy, and spared her

or himself; but with her coming towards him, dressed as I had seen her last, and with her big brown eyes staring wide at me, and looking as if she hated me already, there was not much use contradicting it by a single word again. She went towards him, and put her arms about his neck, and drew the bruised head to her side, and smoothed the short white hair upon it.

'Yes, this is my father,' she said; 'what are you going to do with him, David?'

I looked from her to him.

'I don't know,' I answered; 'it's not my business to hurt him, or to give him up—or—or anything.'

'He did not steal that bundle—I gave it him. I brought it from London for him,' she explained, in a low voice; 'it contains clothes which he was to change for this dreadful prison dress.'

'Good Lor! You knew he was going to escape?'

'Yes, I did,' she confessed.

'How was that?'

'Some one came to her at Whitechapel, and

told her so,' explained the father, 'and to ask her to be ready for me any night after the twenty-second.   A man out of his time sneaked that message to her for me, with the prison brutes never a bit the wiser.   Oh, no !'

He almost · smiled, until a twinge of pain brought him to his miserable self again.

'You've worked it well between the lot of you,' I said, rubbing the bumps upon my forehead, and feeling lost and silly at all this.

'Do you call it well?' he downright hissed at me ; 'to be crippled like this, and with no power to move hand or foot—to be dragged back presently to the cruel slavery of a life like mine !   Fourteen full years of it now, too, by God !   Think of it, man—think of it !'

I was thinking of it already, and it was making me feel very miserable, with Betsy's brown eyes watching me all the while.

'Yes, it's bad enough,' I said ; 'it's precious bad, I know.   But haven't you deserved it?'

'Perhaps I have,' he muttered.   'But there's lots to be said on my side, for with no one ever caring for me, or being better than myself, I

grew to this, of course. Betsy,' he said, turning
to his daughter, 'who is this—this giant of a
man ?'

'Mr. Costerbadie—he lives in this house—
where I lodge.'

'Very poor, ain't you?' he asked, sharply
now.

'Yes, very poor,' I said.

'And honest,' added Betsy.

'Ay, he's had a better start than I had, I'll be
bound,' said Watson.

'And generous,' concluded Betsy, and I felt
myself blushing all over as she went on ; 'a
good, warm-hearted fellow, father, who is my
friend, and who will be your friend for my sake,
even at some risk ; who will hide you, and pro-
tect you somehow till you're strong again, and
not give you up as any coward would.'

I was very dull, but hardly quite as dull as
not to see the drift of this, for all the way in
which she put it ; and not to see the danger of
it either to the lot of us ; to her especially, who
was very much upon my mind, I tell you, sir—

more than she could possibly think, considering the little time I'd known her.

Yes, I saw all the danger—but this was Betsy's father. And I knew Betsy's father was a blackguard, and not worth thinking of over-much or getting into trouble for, but I said, slowly.

'I'll hide you, if I can.'

'God bless you, Davie!' cried Betsy, with trembling lips and tears springing in her eyes—so quick, that I could have cried myself just to keep her company.

'I don't think as how He will for taking care of him,' I said, pointing to my father; 'and it isn't for his sake, but for yours, I'll chance getting into prison along with him. That's all.'

The convict looked from me to Betsy curiously, and then from Betsy to me again.

'It's not a bit of use,' he said at last, and he groaned hard again as he said it; 'where could this chap hide me where I shouldn't be pounced upon half an hour afterwards? Is there such a place in Portland?' he asked.

'I'll try and find one.'

'But is there?'

'I don't think there is. Still, I'll do my best.
You're hurt, you see, and——'

'Yes, yes, that's it,' he answered; 'that's the
cruel mischief of it. If I had been as well and
strong as I was yesterday, I might have got
away.'

'You might,' I said, doubtfully.

'And now I get you and Betsy into trouble
instead.'

'And Betsy's been a good girl all her life,' I
put in here.

'How do you know?' he asked.

'She's told me so.'

The man actually laughed at this, and patted
the hands that were clasped about his neck—
laughed so loudly, that had not Leah and the
rest of them been sound sleepers they must have
heard him in their rooms.

'Here's a man with faith in you, Betsy, and
believes every word you say, and takes it down
for gospel truth—and which it is,' he said, turning suddenly to me, 'for I have kept her away
from Dick Watson all my life, and so have

kept her good.   That's something, ain't it?'

'Yes.'

'But I was getting tired of that,' he went on;
'and when her letters reached me, now and
then, and were full of pity for me, and were
clever letters, too, that told me she was brisk
and sharp, and so on, I thought if I could get
away she would be of mighty help to me.'

'In—what?' I asked.

'In what I have been brought up to all my
life, and am only clever in myself,' he cried, as
if in spite now; 'do you think I can begin anything else at my age, you big idiot?'

Betsy had turned very pale, and the hands
about his neck were trembling very much.

'Mine was a different view of life, father,' she
whispered; 'it was of a place away from here,
where you and I might have begun very humbly
but worthily—something!   I thought if I could
get you away—if I only could—I——'

'That'll do,' he answered, hoarsely, 'I don't
want to hear it.   It's a picture, but it ain't
reality.   There's no more good in it than in me.'

And yet there was some good in this waste of

a man, and it came out, too, in a queerish way—
and where I least expected it. And this is how
it came out.

He looked up suddenly to Betsy.

'Do you mind leaving us for a quarter of an
hour, and going to your room? I want to talk
to this man.'

Betsy looked surprised.

'You can trust me with him, can't you?' he
asked, almost fretfully.

'Oh! yes.'

'And if he gave me up—why, Betsy, it
wouldn't matter much. You're saved, he's saved.
and it's only the old life again for me; and if
we get away,' he added, fiercely, 'it means,
mind, my thief's life, with you to help me always.
None of your weeping and wailing penitence for
me; it isn't in my line, and I won't have it.
There !'

Betsy shivered and moved away.

'We will talk of this presently, you and I together,' she answered, 'and with God's help.'

'Very well. But go away now—and, Betsy—'

'Yes.'

'Kiss me, will you?' he growled out; 'there, now hook it.'

As Betsy went softly upstairs, Dick Watson scuffled to his feet, put his arm through mine again, and said, in a thick, low voice,

'Come on, gov'ner! Take me away, get me out of this.'

'I don't know where to take you.'

'Back to prison, you dolt! Don't you see I'm only fit for that?'

'Oh! I see that plain enough,' I answered.

'And that's where I am going; I won't have her brought into the scrape. I won't have you. Do you hear? don't you understand?' he cried; 'if I could have got away, I'd have altered my mind now.'

'You're going to give yourself up?'

'Something like it. Come on! Let's get out of your house, I can't breathe in it somehow.'

'But—Betsy?' I asked, as we walked from the house together.

'I have said good-bye to her. You can tell her to-morrow I wasn't going to get her into trouble, and that life with me would have been

all I said just now. You need not,' he said,
' talk about my repentance, or any of that hum-
bug; but for all that, Costerbadie, my pluck
failed me at the last. She's better without me.'

We were in the dark high-road together, and
making towards the higher ground, at a slow
and painful rate for him. His arm was like a
lump of iron upon mine, as he leaned with all his
weight upon it.

' You'll never be able to go much further,
man,' I said, ' but I daresay I can carry you.'

' I'll go till I drop,' he answered, between his
teeth, ' and taking our time we shall be able to
do it. I'm in no particular hurry!' and here he
laughed again, like a man who had no end of
fun in him, and was letting some of it off now,
like steam.

Presently he said,

' You don't persuade me to alter my mind ?'

' No.'

' For Betsy's sake, ain't it ?'

' Yes ; that's it.'

' Just as for Betsy's sake you'd have tried to
hide me for a time ?'

'Yes, exactly.'

'Not a bad sort, you,' he muttered, 'and with some sorrow in you even for a fellow like me, though you don't show it much.'

'I'm not sorry for you,' I said, bluntly enough; but he did not seem to take any notice.

'Tell her I was determined to go back to prison, will you, Costerbadie?'

'She'll think I have taken you there, and will hate me after this,' I said.

'She will soon understand,' he replied; 'she will see it as clear as day, and bear in mind all I said to her just now. She's not as dull as you are.'

'Don't you think she'll follow us when the quarter of an hour is up?'

'Ah! she may; let us get on a bit faster. Hark—what's that?'

We stopped to listen. There came the grind, grind of heavy feet in the distance and coming down the hill.

'Two of them!' he said, after a minute's pause: 'two of the warders.'

'Perhaps not.'

· As if I didn't know that infernal tread by this time! as if I hadn't heard it day after day, year after year! Catch hold of my collar, will you? Quick!'

'What for?'

'You've found me, and are dragging me back,' he cried. 'That's five pounds in your pocket, for your loyalty to the Crown; it's always five pounds' reward. Don't you understand?'

'Yes—but Betsy! Oh! Lord's sake, what will she think of me now?'

'The five pounds is for her; she will not have a penny when she gets back to London. Give it to her, as a little present from me!'

'But——'

'Man, it's your only chance of not being dragged in as my accomplice; it's her only chance too. Catch hold, you fool!'

1 held him by the collar, and then the prison men were before us—two black shadows of men, who carried guns under their arms. As they approached, Watson said to me, in a loud voice,

'You need not hold as tight as that unless

you want to choke me; I'm coming quiet enough,
ain't I?—and here's the cursed slops to help
you.'

The men were facing us now, with their guns
very handy for shooting us both down.

'Watson!' cried one, 'and out of prison!'

'Ah! and caught again,' said Watson. 'Haven't
they missed me yet?'

'No, hanged if they have!' growled the
officer; 'and who's the man that's caught you?'

'David Costerbadie, quarryman,' I said.

'Where did you find him?'

'On the Chesil bank,' answered Watson for
me, 'and the big brute has been jumping on me
to keep me still. He's nearly done for me.'

'Serve you right,' was all the officer's reply.

And that's the shabby way, sir, I got Dick
Watson's daughter out of trouble, and it was a
long while before she forgave me, or understood
it, or would see anything but a double face in
me; and when she did see it all clearly I was
very unhappy, and that seemed to bring it
round pretty quick, and open her eyes of a sud-

den to the truth of it. Opened her eyes by little and little, too, to the fact that I was fond of her, and so she did not go back to Whitechapel ever any more, but found work to do in the town until I got into full work soon afterwards myself, and on the strength of it got married. That was two years before Dick Watson died in Portland prison.

He never got out of gaol to begin his new life, or take up his old one, and I think it was just as well, He had done a good turn in his life in leaving Betsy to herself; and the day before he died, when Betsy was allowed to see him, and say good-bye to him, he was very proud of that.

'It's one to me, Betsy, now they've come to the long reckoning,' were the last words he said to my good lady, sir.

TO BE CALLED FOR.

TO BE CALLED FOR.

CHAPTER I.

I DO not know why I should keep this story to myself—to myself and second self, more correctly speaking—any longer. There is nigh upon a score of years between the time of its happening and now, and all the harm the telling of it might have done is as dead and gone as Uncle Samuel is. But to begin at the beginning— which is ship-shape and suits me, being an orderly man always.

My uncle Samuel was my guardian, my father and uncle rolled into one, and took care of me after my own father was drowned. My mother was Uncle Samuel's sister, and became his housekeeper after father's death, attended to

her brother's business when he was out at sea,
put up with all his bad tempers when he was on
shore, and was 'a perfect slave to the old brute,'
it was said in Deal, though my mother was
only a hard working woman, and Sam Nangle
was not exactly a brute. However, my mother
did not live to see my brother at his worst—that
was in the latter years of his life, when he lost
the proper use of his limbs, and had to creep
about the house, clinging to the walls and
furniture, or to toddle down the street with a
couple of crutches which would always go very
wide apart, and which he was never able to use
with any fair amount of grace. At this period
of his career Samuel Nangle was certainly trying, and no one was more certain of that than
myself, his nephew Martin Townsend, at your
service. The most trying time was when I was
about five-and-twenty years of age, and mother
had been dead fifteen out of them. Then he *was*
a trouble to most folk who had anything to do
with him, to me in particular, to whom the care
of the 'Flying Fish' inn, and of the 'Flying Fish'
steam-tug, and of my uncle, the proprietor of

both these Flying Fish, had come by way of natural sequence, as the saying is.

'Not that you're going to have my little tug, when I'm dead and gone, Martin,' my uncle would say, 'they're both too good for you, and I haven't slaved and toiled and moiled all these blessed years to fatten a lazy hunks like you. Don't expect anything from my death, or you'll be more out of your reckoning than you have ever been in your life. You've been too pig-headed, too stuck up, too damned silly to please me, and you must take the consequences. And I hope before you die, Martin, and when you find yourself in the workhouse, that you'll be sorry you didn't treat me better when you had somebody to see after you, and to keep a house over your soft head. There, get out.' And I got out accordingly, and left him to his own company in the little room at the back of the bar, where nobody came now to smoke a pipe or drink a glass of grog with him, my uncle having insulted everybody all round long ago, and lost all his customers, who would not come and spend money and get drunk in his back parlour, to be

I 2

told they were fools and asses, and encum-
brances on the face of the earth, and gibbering,
slobbering idiots, who knew no more about
Deal, or ships, or the sea than his spittoon
there.

It was Uncle Samuel's idea—and I am rather
disposed to think that *all* uncles have a weakness this way—that no one knew anything save
himself, that no one had ever done anything
that was worth mentioning except himself, that
no one had ever been so wise, so careful, so
far-seeing, so lucky, so plucky as he, and it was
his great affliction now that, though everybody
knew this as well as he did, there was no one
to say it to his face like a man, or give him any
credit for it.   He knew that was human nature,
for he knew everything, but he sat in his big
chair by the fire and cursed human nature for
all that, and, when tired of cursing human
nature in the abstract, he would set to work
cursing me.

Well, yes, a dreadful man in many ways, I
own it.   There was not much disguising of it
in Deal, though I did my best to keep the old

man's name sweet in Bilge Street, where he
lived.

'Why you don't cut and run from him, I
can't make out,' was said to me by way of
sage advice. 'The way you're treated, too. It's
abominable!'

But I could not cut and run from so helpless
an old man. He was so terribly alone, and my
mother's brother, too, who had taken care of us
when father went to the bottom of the sea. My
uncle told me about twice a day I was stopping
for what I could get—what would come to me
after he was gone; but he had already warned
me there would be nothing for my share, and I
knew that lawyers had been sent for, and his
will made long ago, and I was out of it. Uncle
Samuel had one virtue—he was always charm-
ingly frank—'infernally rude,' some people said
—and he led me distinctly to understand that I
was 'out of it' for many reasons that he was
not going to explain to a jabbering parrot like
me, who would go and tell all Deal half-an-hour
after I had heard them. Sometimes I fancied
that he wanted me to get away, though what

he would have done without me heaven knows,
I do not. But then I am a little conceited, like
my uncle. He always said I was stuck up, and,
if so, it was in the family. Whether Uncle
Samuel was rich or poor was a matter of grave
speculation to me, and more than me. It was
generally considered that he was a rich man—
that he must have made a lot of money, and
have a rare long stocking somewhere. If the
' Flying Fish' inn had not been a profitable
speculation, the ' Flying Fish' tug had been,
and he in the days of his health and strength
had certainly been a shrewd fellow, and not
overburdened in any way by principles. He
had had his trials, certainly—he had even been
tried for smuggling—but the tug had brought
him in considerable profits, and he was invari-
ably so early at a wreck that there were a few
evil-minded folk to fancy he must have arranged
the wreck beforehand, which, of course, was not
always possible. And he had never been afraid
of work—downright hard, awful work, in the
face of the storm, and of the death which the
storm threatened, and Dare Devil Sam had

been his nickname in the town for years, before his dare-devilship stumped about the streets on crutches.

I remember the last winter I spent with my uncle very well; it was a memorable season, and his manners were peculiar, even for him. He was getting worse and worse, they said in Bilge Street; the neighbours were not safe from scoffs and taunts when they passed him in the street, and the little children shrieked at sight of him and ran away, though their big brothers made up for this by throwing stones. In the corner of the bar-parlour he was only bearable when fast asleep, or after his fourteenth glass of grog, when he would become boastful of his past exploits, or maudlin over the helplessness which hindered him from repeating them. Even in his miserable old age he seemed to love the sea, and to be more keen and clear in his faculties when he could hear it roaring and breaking on the beach, with the wind shrieking like a woman. One winter's night, when the elements were going it in real earnest, he sat huddled in his big chair, with his legs on a footstool, and a

warm rug round him, listening with grave satisfaction to the storm.

' Had I been as young as you are, I would
have been out in this,' he said to me. ' I
wouldn't have been hulking here scouring pewter
pots.'

I had done my scouring long ago, but it was
his neat way of putting it.

' It's a roughish night,' I said, not caring to
aggravate him by any defence, now that he was
a little pleasant in his manner.

'I should have had steam up in the "Flying
Fish," and gone. That's where the pull is, for the
ships are sure to go to pieces, or run ashore on
a night like this, as sure as thunder and lightning, death and the devil, boy.'

' Yes, exactly,' I said; 'and you were never
afraid of danger?'

'Afraid!' he roared forth. 'I was never afraid
of anything, you fool, you! I never stopped at
anything, or let anything stop me; what I wanted I had always. If they said I shouldn't have
it, I took it for myself.'

' If who said?'

'What's that to you? And so I've got pretty warm and comfortable, and——'

I ventured to supply a word.

'And happy?'

'No, you wretched, limp, underdone, hair-dresser of a man—not happy. Who could be happy with you? Who could be happy with a blazing pair of legs like these, and with——'

Then he was silent suddenly, and I mixed him another glass of rum-and-water at a peculiar sign he was accustomed to make, with one hand and one eye, and which meant rum and water, hot, with a slice of lemon in it. He did not say any more. He became strangely silent for him; for, when he had not me to talk to, he would talk to himself for hours—talk himself to sleep, and then go on muttering in his dreams in a rare, busy fashion. But that night he grew suddenly still and quiet, and stared before him strangely at a Grace Darling picture on the opposite wall, and continued to stare after I had left him to attend to a customer in the shop, who was a little impatient, and kept tapping so persistently with a piece of money on the pewter-covered counter, that I had quite made up my mind to sauce him for his hurry. But it was not a 'him.' When I had reached the shop, which was down a long passage, and a good distance from the parlour, between which and the shop there were more rooms than one, the 'Flying Fish' inn being a rambling old place, I discovered my customer to be a female, a young female, and a pretty one, too, for all her pale face and big blue staring eyes. I did not know her for one of my neighbours—for anyone in Deal, where I knew everyone by sight, and I was sure she was a foreigner before she spoke a word. Her dress was very dark, but it was peculiar ; her hair was very light, her hat or bonnet seemed rather of a queer shape, and there were two funny little crystal crosses in her ears.

'What can I get you, lady?' I asked at last, as she continued to look at me—to regard me in my turn in the light of a curiosity.

Then she spoke in English, but with a foreign accent, and in a very low tone.

'You cannot be the man,' she said, wonderingly—'you are younger, taller, different altogether. You do not answer the description; you——'

'What man do you want?'

'I wish to see Mr. Samuel Nangle, of the "Flying Fish,"' she answered.

'This is the "Fying Fish," and Mr. Nangle is my uncle.'

'He is alive?'

'Oh, yes.'

'And well?'

'Not well. He has not been well and strong for years, but then he is very old.'

'Yes, I know.'

I was surprised at the extent of her knowledge, but waited for her to inform me of the object of her visit.

'Is he indoors?'

'Yes.'

'Can I see him?'

'Ye—es, I think so,' I said, hesitatingly, 'although it's late in the evening, and he is not particularly nice to visitors, as a rule.'

'He expects me!'

'My—my Uncle Samuel—expects you!' I exclaimed.

'Yes, he has been expecting me for some time,' was the quiet explanation proffered, 'for days, months, years, I daresay. He has been always certain I should come. Why, it was as sure I should call some day as that the sun will rise to-morrow.'

For the first time she smiled, and I liked the look of her when she smiled.

'I'll tell my uncle you have come then,' I said.

'Thank you ; do.'

'Who—who shall I say has called ?'

'Bertha Keefeland. He will know the name.'

'Indeed !'

'Has he never spoken of it to you ?'

'Never.'

'That's strange,' she remarked. 'Has he altered very much of late years ?'

'Yes, very much.'

'People do. Well, tell him I have come, young man.'

I was proceeding in a wondering, dreamlike fashion towards the long, dark passage again, when she called back, and said,

'Is his memory as good as it used to be? Old people forget; my father did, sadly—very sadly.'

Her face shadowed at some reminiscence, and I said,

'I think his memory is pretty good for most things.'

'Still, he may have forgotten,' was the thoughtful comment here; 'the name may have even passed away altogether from his recollection. He never speaks of me, you say?'

'He does not.'

'Perhaps it will be as well to say Caspar Keefeland's daughter.'

'I'll make a point of doing so.'

'And if he's too old, or too ill to see me, I will not worry him,' she continued. 'Only tell him to let me have the sandal-wood box which was left here to be called for.'

'To be called for?'

'Yes. Which my father left with him— which he told him I should fetch some day.'

'Oh! did he?' I said, completely bewildered now, and wondering at all this, and what it meant, and what was to follow. I was borne down by grim forebodings, which closed thick and fast about me as I shambled my way along the dark passage to the inn-parlour.

CHAPTER II.

UNCLE SAMUEL NANGLE was sitting very much
in the same position as I had left him, only he
had dropped his rum-and-water from his hands,
and the glass lay shattered into a hundred
pieces on the floor. He was still staring at the
picture portraying Grace Darling's heroism, or
at a something beyond the picture, very far
away indeed, and which troubled him that
night. I should have fancied in another minute
that he had had a stroke of something, if he
had not said to me very plainly, but huskily, as
I came into the room,

'What is it, Martin?'

'A visitor.'

'A what?'

'A visitor,' I repeated. 'Somebody who

wants to see you, and who has come a long
way to see you, I should say,' was my reply.

'A long way, is it?' he muttered; 'you don't
mean from the grave, Martin? You wouldn't
frighten an old man in that way?'

'Certainly not,' I cried; 'why, is that like me
at any time?'

'Nothing is like you,' he said, slowly and re-
flectively; 'I don't call to mind anybody just
now who was ever such a fool as you are.'

My uncle was coming round to his old manner now, and I was glad of it. His staring fit
was over, and it had scared me just a little. I
had fancied something was going to happen,
having been full of fancies all that day.

'Well, who is it wants to see me?' he asked,
querulously. 'Who's come all of a hurry to ask
after my health, and to wish me joy of it?'

'It's a young girl!'

'Eh?'

'A foreigner—German, without doubt, or
Dutch, perhaps.'

'Eh?'

'A pretty girl, but very pale.'

'Eh? oh! go on. With glass crosses in her ears?'

'Why, yes. But have——'

'And what's her name, Martin?' he asked now, very eagerly.

'Bertha Keefeland!'

'No—no—no—that's a lie. That's a dreadful lie of somebody's,' he roared forth, suddenly. 'I tell you it can't be!'

'Oh! but it is, uncle,' I explained; 'and she's come, she says, for the sandal-wood box which was left here to be called for.'

'There's no sandal-wood box,' he exclaimed, in the same loud key. 'There's no Bertha Keefeland, for she has been dead these six years. There's no——'

And then he fell forward, with a horrible screech, face foremost on the floor, and I ran to him and picked him up, and wiped the dust off his hard, rugged cheeks and forehead, and put him back again in the big chair from which he had pitched out. I was as sorry to see him struck down like that as if I had loved him, or he had loved me a little, and I scuttled into the bar again for

water, for the help of the young woman, who
might run for a doctor for me, or mind my uncle
whilst I ran myself.   But the shop was empty,
and there was no Bertha Keefeland waiting for
me to come back with my uncle's answer to her
message.

CHAPTER III.

THE host of the 'Flying Fish' did not recover
from the fright or the malady which had seized
him. He was one remove nearer to the end of
his time now; I knew as well as possible that he
would never want his crutches any more, and
that one of these fine days or nights he would
be sailing clean away.

He knew it himself, I think, though the
doctor had not warned him. The doctor had
left it to me, who was not likely to be a good
hand at breaking to the old man such news as
that, and who did not care to tell him, and
thought it was as well not to tell him, as
it was not likely to do him any good. I did ask
him if he would like to see the parson, and he
swore at me with such fluency for the suggest-

ion, that I thought for a minute or two he was getting rapidly better. But he wound up in a milder fashion.

'Parsons ain't any good to me,' he said, 'are they?'

'Well, I don't think they are much.'

'I always hated parsons. I haven't seen one of my own accord since I was christened. I've kept out of their way.'

'Yes, you have.'

'I know I have,' he added. 'I could have told the parson a blessed sight more than he could have ever told me. And, besides, salt water doesn't mix with holy water, does it?'

'I don't know.'

'No. You don't know much.'

He did not say any more that day. He was very thoughtful at times now, as he had been on the night when he was spoken to. From the day of his last illness to this—a fortnight afterwards nearly—he had never alluded to the girl who had called at the 'Flying Fish,' and whom I had not set eyes on since that stormy night. And yet I believe he *was* thinking of her a good deal, and of the message she had sent to him by me. Presently I knew he was thinking of her, and could think of nothing else.

One day, and a very long and thoughtful day it was to him, he beckoned me to his bedside with his thick, crooked finger. He had got very hoarse, and there was a difficulty in making out all he said, but I had managed it somehow during the morning and afternoon.

'Martin,' he croaked forth, almost like a raven, ·I don't fancy I'm quite as well as usual to-night.'

'Perhaps it is fancy, uncle?'

'Am I looking as well? I don't want any lies about it!'

'I don't see much difference in you.'

'Then I don't suppose there is. You were never much of a liar, Martin. You have been over-particular that way, and that's bad for a man who means to stick to business, hard and fast.'

'I'm not so sure of that.'

'But I am, and that's enough, ain't it?'

'All right,' I said, although I knew it was all

wrong, and so had begun lying on my own
account. But I did not wish the old gentleman
to get excited over any argument. 'Give him
his own way,' had been the doctor's orders;
'let him say and do what he pleases.'

'I know I am not going to get over this,
Martin,' my uncle said. 'That's all square
enough; and I've had my innings, and don't
grumble. But, Martin, where the devil am I
going to?'

'For mercy's sake, don't go on like this!'

'I didn't reckon on *her* calling for me—on her
waiting for me,' he muttered. 'Fancy her
always with me afterwards. . It's awful!'

'Do you mean——'

Then I came to a full stop, but he understood me.

'Yes, I mean that girl.'

'Bertha Keefeland?'

'Yes, Bertha Keefeland.'

'How can she be waiting for you, uncle?'

'Didn't she come two weeks ago?'

'Why, yes.'

'She came out of her coffin,' he whispered,

· and I was waiting for her that night. She
had been upon my mind all day. I couldn't
get her out of my head. She was troubling it
very much.'

'That's all nonsense,' I cried. 'She was flesh
and blood, I'll swear.'

He shook his head.

'No, she wasn't,' he said ; 'how could she be ?'

I could not reason with him. He was so
convinced to the contrary, and I was perplexed
and goosefleshy. Certainly Bertha Keefeland
had mysteriously disappeared, after giving me
the message to my uncle, but people are always
disappearing and being advertised for, and turning up again. And this might have even been
a practical joke, only—and then I thought of a
sandal-wood box, which was upstairs, and had
been upstairs for years, on the top of a tall,
double chest of drawers belonging to my uncle,
and the mystery of it was beyond my fathoming.

But he let in the light upon it presently, and
it was a red light, warning him of danger—a
light as red as blood.

'She couldn't have been flesh and blood,

Martin,' he went on, slowly; 'for, six years
ago, when you were away in London once, she
came into this house, into that shop downstairs,
just as she did a fortnight since, said she was
Bertha Keefeland, and had called for the box
her father had left with me.'

'Good gracious!'

'She was tall, and thin, and pale, with glass
crosses in her ears, and she knew very little
English, and spoke it very badly. Is that the
girl?'

'It answers the description,' I answered, with
a shudder. 'Well, she has called again, that's
all.'

'Yes, she's certainly called again,' he repeated,
grimly.

'Well, then——'

'But,' he added, with a look which I shall
never forget, and which silenced me at once—a
look which comes to me often and often in my
sleep still, and gives me awful nightmares, 'I
killed her on the night she called to see me
first, and for three days her body lay behind the
big vat in the cellar where the whisky is, until

one dark night I took *it* down to the beach, and the sea carried it away for me, and there was an end of it, I thought. An end! As if there can be an end to things like that—as if she was not to come back some day just as she has done. I feel that's a clean breast of it, Martin, and you're not the man to put a rope round my neck for telling you ; not you.'

'No. Not I.'

I stood and looked at him, and wondered if he were raving at the last—for I did not think there were many more hours of life in him, and his senses might have left him first, as they will do sometimes, perhaps out of politeness. Could it be possible, I thought, that my uncle was a murderer, that this was true, and that the Bertha Keefeland of a fortnight since was a spirit from another world? Were there, after all, such things as ghosts to walk the earth and avenge the deeds which made them so ? To look upon this agitated, earnest old man was to believe it almost. It seemed so awfully like the truth coming from those thin white lips. And presently I did not even doubt it.

'I don't mind telling you the rest of it, Martin
—you'll understand then why I haven't left you
any money in my will. It's more than twenty
years ago when Caspar Keefeland and I were
friends first—when he fell sick one day, in this
very room, and was afraid he should die before
he got back to his native village, and the wife
and baby he had left behind him there. He
travelled a good deal between Russia and
England, and always put up at the "Flying
Fish." The last time I am talking about—when
he was ill, that is—he had brought with him a
box made of sandal-wood, a legacy, he told me,
from a rich relation who had died in London
that year. Before he left Deal, he got the
notion into his head that he should die before
he reached home, and so he asked me to take
care of the box and its contents, being pretty
sure his mates would stick to it if he shouldn't
live to get off shipboard. For some reason, too,
he did not want his wife to know of this at
present. "It'll be a surprise to her some day,"
he said, "and for Bertha. I'll leave it with you
to be called for, Sam," he said; "it's safe with

you as with the Bank of England. Bertha shall
come here for it some day, when she grows to
be a woman—that's time enough. I don't want
for anything now; I may then. I can trust you,
Sam, and I can only trust you, to keep it safe
for her. And, if I should die before I get home,
you'll take it to Germany yourself. Say that's
a promise?" And I said it was a promise. So
it was.'

'Well?' I gasped. 'Go on.'

'But Caspar did get home, though he was
taken worse on the journey. He was never fit
for much work again. He was something like
I've been of late years, lad, I'd heard—a staring
figure-head, a stuffed Guy Fawkes, a scarecrow
of the cussedest. But he sent me one line,
which somebody wrote for him: "*Keep it till
called for*," it said, "*till Bertha comes*," and I kept
it.'

'And she came?'

'Yes. Don't be in a hurry; you're always in
such a beastly hurry,' he said. 'I haven't told
you what was in the box.'

'Did you know?'

'One night I broke it open.'

'Oh!'

'I wasn't particular; I never was over-particular,' he said; 'and I wanted to be sure what Caspar was making all this fuss about. And there were diamonds and large gold bits of foreign money, and then more diamonds in the queerest settings. They fetched a lot of money.'

'Did you sell them?'

'I was in difficulties,' he continued. 'I had been tried for smuggling. There were heavy expenses for my defence, and heavier fines to pay, and I wanted money badly. When I wanted money badly, I always got it somehow, and Keefeland's jewels came in handy.'

'That was dreadful.'

'Old Keefeland took no notice, and nobody called for the property. I thought he must have forgotten to tell anybody about it,' he went on; 'that he had gone off for good without telling wife or child—that he had thought I might as well have the things as anybody else. He was so very fond of me.'

'I wonder why that was?' I said.

'You mind your own business, and wonder at what I've got to tell you,' growled my uncle. 'That'll be quite enough,' he added, with a shudder, which lasted so long that I thought he would shudder himself out of the world, and so an end to him before his story. But he suddenly rallied, and went on—'One night, though, she did come—Bertha Keefeland, at the same time, on the same sort of night as the last, with the wind roaring down the street, and shaking all the windows. She walked into the place, and asked me for the box just as she asked you, and I would have sooner seen her ghost then. God knows I did not know what to do. I had sold the jewels and the foreign money. I could only see a prison for me, and—and I was always a desperate fellow in my heart of hearts. I asked her to step into the next room—the room close to the bar, which I always keep locked. You guess now why? and—and—but I've told you all the rest. You know—you know! and you have seen her risen from the dead. And she will come once more for me, too; we shall

see her walk into this room again, you and I
together; now, mark my words. That's what
I am waiting for.'

'Oh, don't get that into your head.'

'And I shouldn't like you to be out of the
way when she calls for me instead of for the
box. I'm to be called for now, so don't leave
me, Martin, not for a moment, there's a dear,
good lad.'

CHAPTER IV.

WAS Uncle Nangle, after all, so very bad a
specimen of a murderer, or had he learned repentance after his fashion, and understood what
remorse was—what atonement? He told me
before he died that he had left all his money to
the nearest of kin of Caspar Keefeland, whoever
he or she might be; that it was on his conscience
—or what he thought his conscience—that this
should be the destination of his money, which
was not half as much as people thought he had
scraped together. He told me something more
than this. That he had made himself as hard,
cruel, and brute-like as he could to me, so that
I should be glad, rather than sorry, when he
was gone—so that there should seem a natural
reason in his strong dislike of me for leaving
the money somewhere else. Even after his

death no one would suspect him of so babyish a thing as restitution, he hoped. He would have liked to die 'hard as nails,' but it was not to be. He could not have his own way in everything. Who can ?

'I wasn't half as bad as I tried to be, Martin, that's all,' he said to me the next night, when he was lingering on still. 'I wanted you to hate me. But you wouldn't.'

His voice was a long way off now—he was much weaker—he could hardly lift his hand from the bed-clothes. He was not likely now to spin me any more of his long yarns. That very night, again, I was trying hard to think it *was* a yarn, and nothing more.

Later on, he said, in a half-absent way, and yet in a way that was strangely impressive to me,

'She hasn't called for me yet. What a time she keeps me waiting!'

I put my hand on his, which was fidgeting restlessly outside the bed-clothes, and said,

'Don't think anything more of such nonsense. If it's all true you've told me——'

' If !' he murmured, indignantly.

'Think of that a bit, and how sorry you are now.'

He stared at me like a man resenting my advice; then he made a sudden effort to sit up in bed, and failed; lastly, he clutched my hand with both his own.

' I'm—called—for !' he said. ' Here she is, by God—at last !'

He gave a long sigh, shut his eyes, and died; and the breath had not been out of his worn old body half a minute before, to my horror and amazement, the door was slowly and softly opened, and there stole into the room the young woman, or the ghost of the young woman, who a fortnight since had told me that her name was Bertha Keefeland.

I thought, in that moment, it was the ghost of Bertha—a ghost with glass earrings !—for my nerves were unstrung; my uncle was just dead, and his story was not four-and-twenty hours old. I cowered from her among the bed-curtains. I was not half a man for the next five minutes. I could hear my heart pounding away inside me like a steam-hammer.

Here a very natural woman's voice exclaimed :

' Dead ! Oh, is he dead, my poor old father's friend ?'

I looked round the curtains at her ; she was bending over him with tears of interest in her blue eyes. She had put a little hand upon his cold, hard forehead. She was so uncommonly unlike a ghost that I could not believe in Uncle Samuel's story any more. His brain had given way in his old age, and that was the explanation of it. An odd coincidence or two—life is all coincidences—had helped to make the yarn remarkable, and that was all.

' How long has he been dead !' she asked, in a whisper, and as if afraid she might wake him.

' Just a minute,'

' I heard in Deal that he was very ill, and I came to you at once. I could not make anybody hear in the shop, so I thought 1 would not run away again, but come upstairs to where the footsteps were. I guessed what was happening,' she said, sorrowfully, ' and I had hoped to see him once before his death ; to give him poor father's message—father's thanks.'

'You—you have never seen him before then?'

'Never.'

'You have never been in England before this year?' I asked.

'Never.'

'And you are Bertha Keefeland—Caspar Keefeland's daughter?'

'Oh, yes.'

'Poor old Uncle Nangle,' I murmured, looking at him, 'how your mind wandered at the last, to be sure!'

'Did he speak of me?' she asked.

'Yes. I should rather think he did.'

'My coming to England distressed him a deal, reminding him, I daresay, so much of father.'

'Hum! perhaps it did.'

'"Don't tell him everything too suddenly—he's old like me," said my father, before he died,' she continued; '"give him plenty of time to think matters over—say you'll call again, or anything." And when, a fortnight ago, I heard him shriek out after you had taken in my

message to him, I felt I had been too hasty, and
I crept away at once, giving him more time, as
father wished.'

'Oh! I see.'

'See what?'

'That your father was a wonderfully considerate man. And yet——'

'And yet?' she repeated.

'My uncle never seemed exactly the man
for anybody to be considerate about,' I concluded.

'My father liked him very much always. I
don't think you could have understood your uncle,'
she said, thoughtfully, almost reproachfully.

'Well, I suppose I didn't,' I confessed.

'I have a little more to say—but,' she added,
with a shiver, 'is there any reason I should say
it here? Any reason we should stop here
longer?'

'No. Please come downstairs,' I answered.

We went to the bar parlour, where she sat
down in my uncle's chair, and looked hard at
me. She was a very pretty German girl, I
thought.

'Now, about the box,' she said, 'I don't wish to trouble you concerning it till after your uncle's funeral. I will simply ask you to take extra care of it, now that it is in your sole custody, and not in the good man's upstairs, who has held it in faithful trust for me so long. I may tell you even there are jewels of considerable value in it, and I am very poor. That may interest you, perhaps—for my sake,' she added, with a faint little smile.

'To be sure,' I answered, heartily, 'and that it does. But——'

She waited for me to proceed, looking at me anxiously.

'But before his death my uncle spoke of those jewels, and said—whether in his sober senses or out of them, the Lord knows, Miss Keefeland— that—that,' I stammered forth, 'he had turned the jewels into money.'

'Why should he have done that?'

'As a kind of loan, perhaps,' I suggested. 'His statement was not very clear, and, as there was a ghost mixed up with it, I could not make it out exactly; but the long and the short of it is, he has left all his money, every scrap of it, to you.'

' To me !'

' To the next-of-kin of Caspar Keefeland. That is you, I hope?' I asked, nervously, ' or the poor old boy has made a pretty mess of it.'

' Yes; it is I.'

' That's all right.   I'm glad.'

' But you are his nephew—should be his heir,' she exclaimed.   ' What has he left you ?'

' He has not thought of me in any way.'

' Oh, that is wrong !'

' No; I think it is right,' I answered.

' How can it be ?'

' How can anything be ?' I said, in my desper-ate bewilderment. ' Don't try to make out anything just yet, Miss Keefeland, please. If you had only come before—years and years before !'

' I was taking care of father, and he only spoke of the box a few months ago, and just before he died. It had passed out of his memory completely, he said. He was a very forgetful man; and,' she added, thoughtfully, 'as he had many troubles, it was just as well.'

' Yes,' I assented, ' I should say so.'

' I should not have been surprised if the box had been missing altogether,' she remarked. ' I was prepared to hear you tell me that when I first called here.'

' Why?' I asked, cautiously.

' There was some one who knew the box was here—my father's second wife, and a Bertha Keefeland, too. My father had told her of it once. He remembered that he had spoken of it to her.'

I felt a creeping up my back now.

' Your father's second wife,' I repeated, in a husky whisper.

' Yes. He married her a year or two after he had come back from Deal for the last time. Married her for a nurse, and to take care of me, left motherless. And she was too wild and passionate and—and—wicked. She deserted him.'

' What—what has become of her?'

' I don't know. She left a letter on the table

one night, stating that she could bear her life no
longer, and must go away from him and me.
She was then about the age I am,' Bertha added,
thoughtfully. 'She was much too young for father.
He was very fond of her, though ; after she had
left him he made me dress like her, and wear
ornaments like her, too. It was a strange
fancy.'

Yes. I saw the story now, I thought, from
its shadowy beginning to its end. The young
wife of Caspar Keefeland, after deserting her
husband, had come to the ' Flying Fish ' for the
sandal-wood box, had come with a lying message
from Caspar, and met her death in coming.

Uncle Nangle's confession was true, after all.
Bit by bit I sifted it out. The old man had
killed the wrong Bertha Keefeland, and year
after year it became more and more plain to me
—more and more of a terrible tale of temptation
and cupidity. Let me turn away from it for
good—it will be known only to Bertha and me
until this hand is still which puts the record on
paper.

Bertha is my wife. She came into my uncle's

money, and, as she insisted upon sharing it with me, we made up our minds just to share our lives together as well, and so round the story like an orange.

And the moral of this story always strikes me as a queer one. If Uncle Nangle had not murdered Casper Keefeland's second wife, I should have never married Bertha Keefeland, and been happy for the rest of my days. Bertha says I must not put it down as murder, but then she always looks on the bright side of everything.

TOO MUCH OF A DISCOVERY.

TOO MUCH OF A DISCOVERY.

AFTER mature deliberation, I have thought it better to commit my statement to writing, lest when I get into years some of the facts may escape my memory, or people should assert that my mind had given way, and I was only fit for Bethlehem Hospital. Extraordinary as this bare recital of my narrative may be, still let me record here the plain unvarnished truth of it, leaving the world to think what it likes of the matter, and having at least eased my mind of a weighty burden. This by way of preface—by way of confession, if you will—of Selina Sarah Stonehouse, of Vox Stellarum Villa, Sydenham-on-the-Rise.

1 am Selina Sarah Stonehouse, spinster. I
reside with my brother Erasmus Pascal Stonehouse, bachelor. We have been together all
our lives, the early decease of our parents having set us side by side together with an united
income, which may be designated as comfortable, if limited. It is extremely doubtful if
Erasmus or I—especially Erasmus—have ever
given a thought to living apart from each other,
to forming those domestic ties which render the
separation of brother and sister a thing, as a
rule, to be desired.

Speaking particularly for Erasmus, I have no
doubt whatever that giving himself in marriage
to anyone, or having anyone given in marriage
to him, has not, up to the present period, entered
into his head. He has not had a moment's time
to think about it, and, as he is now exactly
sixty-three years of age, I believe it is probable
that he will continue to the end of his days to
regard the tender passion as a fugitive something belonging to poetry and dream-books, and
not to active life—active life, speaking figur-
atively, of course, for Erasmus has only been

once out of his own house and garden since he was five-and-thirty, and that was to the funeral of his old friend Mithridates Mould, who sent his compliments to him on his dying bed, and hoped he would make it convenient to come.

As for the tender passion as regards myself, I am only fifty-seven now, and youth is hardly far enough in the background to state with any certainty what may ultimately ensue to one's career. But as yet my heart has not fluttered very sympathetically to the emotions, for the sad reason that no one—with the exception of Professor Cinders—has fluttered sympathetically round me. Of the professor I will speak presently, for he is a prime mover in this story, alas! and rests, as it were, like a shadow on my life—the shadow of a little round-shouldered man with goggle eyes, who wears slippers and takes snuff, and is sixty-five, if he is a day. I speak with acrimony, and possibly I have cause, but he *is* sixty-five. I have seen it in 'People of the Day,' though what the editor wanted to put *him* in for, and leave Erasmus out, is only to be explained by that new theory of 'Chicken and

Champagne,' which a young man on the superior
papers has lately promulgated with much solid
airiness of style.

My brother Erasmus is scientific—intensely
scientific. He takes it from his grandfather on
the mother's side, who died scientifically. If
Erasmus had given his talents fair play, instead
of diving into the abstrusest subjects, and
seldom rising to the surface again, I believe my
brother would years ago have been the talk of
all the learned societies in Europe. The wonder
of them would be a more appropriate expression. The talk of them he may have been, for
he used to write to them twice a week in various languages, and refute by positive proof
almost everything they said, defying them to
answer him coherently, which they seldom did,
coherently or incoherently, for the matter of
that. Such was the envy my brother created
at one period in the world of science, the reader
perceives; but Erasmus bore up bravely, and
studied on, feeling that the spirit of research,
like virtue, was its own reward, and, encouraged
by my sympathy, he was content with it. All

the same if he were not, it may be said, but I
simply state the fact.

Vox Stellarum Villa was a few years ago the
resort of the numerous learned minds who were
resident in Sydenham, where my brother read a
paper once a week to all the friends and acquaintances he could possibly persuade to come
and hear him.   In these evenings he impercep-
tibly influenced modern thought, like the pebble
in the water-brook, with the ripples widening
and ever widening, and so forth—a happy meta-
phor, but a trifle spoiled by everybody using it.
I presume my brother Erasmus would not at
any time have been generally considered cheerful society.   To speak metaphorically again, he
did not make the welkin ring with his hilarity.
He was conversational, he was fond of reading
aloud; but as his conversation and his readings
were all of the deepest calibre, and full of
logarithms, decimal fractions, parallaxes, and
angles of refraction and reflection, they were
beyond my finite intelligence to fathom, and I
was simply content to reverence him.

But he was not cheerful.   He rose early, and

perambulated the garden in his dressing-gown
till breakfast time—walking very fast, with a
pencil and note-book in his hand, lest any idea
should dart away from him before he could get it
on his tablets.   When he was on friendly terms
with Professor Cinders—who lives next door—
he used to hold long converse with him.   Professor Cinders rose early also, and perambulated
his garden in very much the same fashion as
Erasmus, and when they both came to a stand-
still, to see those two learned heads, both in
skull-caps, and both resting their chins on the
top of the brick wall dividing their gardens, and
both arguing their hardest on the differential
calculus, or the volatility of comets, was to
apprehend they might eventually come to blows
in the pursuit of science.   And that fear arose
in my breast chiefly on account of Erasmus,
who was excitable under opposition.   Professor
Cinders was, on the contrary, heavy and phleg-
matic, but dreadfully aggravating; and from my
chamber window—which commands a fine view
of the back garden—I have often dreaded lest
the goggle eyes of the professor should be

mercilessly 'bashed' into his system by an impulsive, but neighbourly, fist.

At breakfast Erasmus was accustomed to read all the scientific papers which had arrived by the first post; after breakfast he sat down to contradict the major portion of the contents; at dinner he was exceedingly thoughtful, wondering what he had written or what he had forgotten to write; in the evening Professor Cinders would call, or some of his learned friends, and they would retire to his study at the top of the house, there to remain till the middle of the night, when they would let themselves out softly, like conspirators or burglars, for fear of waking me or the servants out of our first sleep.

Hence, you see, my life has been somewhat dull and neutral tinted, but a change came suddenly, and the even tenor of my maiden way became upheaved with earthquakes. And this is how it all occurred.

In the beginning of the winter of some three or four years since there was to be detected a perceptible difference in my brother Erasmus's demeanour. From a studious and absent-mind-

M 2

ed man, he became by degrees—and by very
rapid and startling degrees—a marble statue,
with scarcely the gift of speech, and with an
unpleasant habit of sitting with his mouth open.

'Erasmus, for goodness' sake don't stare like
that,' I said to him, sharply, on the first occasion,
and he closed his mouth at once, and answered,
very meekly,

'I'm not staring, Selina.'

He was not aware of it, but it was none the
less a dreadful falsehood. And five minutes
afterwards he was glaring so dreadfully at the
pink bow on the top of my cap that I thought it
was on fire.

'Oh, dear! Erasmus Pascal, you make me
shockingly nervous. *Is* anything the matter?'
I exclaimed.

'Yes, something is the matter,' he replied.

'Good gracious! Where?'

'Something is very much the matter,' he said,
in a deep whisper, 'and it must not go any
further.'

'Well, dear—what——'

'1 will tell you to-morrow. I am going to my

study directly. I don't want to be interfered
with, Selina. 1 shall not require you, or Mary,
or Jane'—our servant-maids, I may remark here
—'to come upstairs every five minutes to tell
me dinner is ready. When I want dinner, I'll
riug for it. At present all I require is perfect
repose in the establishment.'

Erasmus had been on the verge of many
remarkable discoveries during the course of his
life, but had always, at the eleventh hour, been
forestalled by some one with a similar idea, or
had his idea completely stolen from him. Sad
experience of human kind had rendered him
secretive—turned his trust and confidence, even
in me, into a fear of betrayal—and he would
tell me nothing then. When I questioned him
too closely, as time went on, he would respond,
'Anon, anon,' like a character in an Elizabethan
drama, and glide out of the room backwards,
waving one hand towards me.

There came a complete change in all his
habits. He left off writing to the learned societies, their printed papers remained uncut upon
the table, unless they were papers on electricity,

when he would devour them along with his ham
and eggs, and laugh silently to himself, until
something went the wrong way and nearly
choked him, which would bring him round a
little. He left off his *conversaziones*, and sent
down apologies to his numerous friends who
called, stating that he was particularly busy
just then, and could not spare a moment of his
time. He declined to see Professor Cinders,
who was not to be turned so quickly off the
premises, and who sent word back that he
would wait till he was disengaged, which he
would do for hours, playing five-card cribbage
with me, night after night, till I was afraid the
servants would think we were engaged. And
Professor Cinders *was* attentive at that period of
my career, took pity on my loneliness, discoursed
with me about Erasmus, and of the probability
of brain-softening having set in with alarming
suddenness, talked of my dull existence, and of
his lonely widower's home, with six grown-up
daughters always quarrelling and shrieking;
talked of the comfort I was to him, and how
glad he was to get out of his own house.

Very late at night, when the supper things had not been cleared away, Erasmus would come creeping down and say, feebly,

'Ah! Cinders, are you here? How d'ye do?'

'I'm very well, Stonehouse; I hope you are.'

'I'm famous, thank you,' my brother would reply; 'any news?'

The professor would tell him the news, to which he would listen for a few minutes over his supper-plate, and then there would come that fixed glare at my top-bow, or at the place where the professor would have had a top-bow had he worn one, and the lower jaw of Erasmus would begin slowly to descend.

Once Professor Cinders, a bold and resolute man, appealed to him in the hall, when Erasmus was seeing him off the premises. Of course, I could not see the professor off the premises at my time of life—I mean at that hour of the night.

'Stonehouse,' he said, decisively, 'you'll allow an old friend to say you're killing yourself.'

'Pooh, nonsense!'

'You'll also allow an old friend the privilege

of saying you're making a fool of yourself,
Stonehouse.'

'Pray don't mention it.'

'And I may add, it's not particularly friendly
to keep us all in the dark as to, as to—what the
devil your game is.'

'You won't be in the dark much longer,'
Erasmus said, meaningly.

'That's well. I'm glad of it, for one. For
upon my honour, Stonehouse, it's a very difficult
thing to know what to do with one's evenings,
when there's no club within a rational distance,
no scientific mind to commune with, nothing
but your sister, and an old cribbage-board and
four damned lucifers for pegs.'

I was not listening, but the words could not
escape me. I felt my colour rising at his mean-
ness—for the lucifers were his own suggestion,
as the pegs had got mislaid somewhere.

'Cinders, I am on the verge of a great discovery,' 1 heard Erasmus say, in a stage aside,
'one of the greatest discoveries—decidedly the
greatest discovery of the age. Presently the
world will be considerably thunderstruck, and

its whole social fabric shaken to its centre.'

'Good God—it's fireworks!' exclaimed the professor; 'it's a new gunpowder, or something.'

'No, it's nothing explosive—though,' he added, with a little squeaking laugh, 'it will burst up a good many pet theories. Good-night, Cinders.'

'But——'

'You shall know all anon,' interrupted my brother, 'not now; and you'll excuse my standing any longer in this draught, with three buttons off my dressing-gown. Good-night, good-night.'

Erasmus returned to the sitting-room, and recommenced his glaring.

'Selina, have you heard what Cinders and I were talking about?' he said.

'Yes; I have heard a little.'

'You have been playing the eavesdropper.'

'I have played at nothing this evening except cribbage, and that I have played with Mr. Cinders for the last time,' I said, loftily.

'Has he been cheating?'

'No—he has not.'

'He would cheat *me* out of my birthright—
my mess of—mess of—something or other—my
discovery. But till it is all worked out *here*,'
tapping his forehead, ' and *there*,' pointing to the
ceiling, but meaning his upstairs laboratory,
' no living soul shall guess what is in store for
this present memorable century. No living,
human, breathing soul, Selina?' he added,
sharply.

' Yes, dear. What is it now ?'

' If you should hear a strange hissing noise in
the middle of the night, it will not be snakes or
the kitchen boiler exceeding its maximum of
steam,' he said : ' it will be my biggest battery
at work.'

' But you are not going to study any more to-
night ?'

' Just for half an hour, while the moon is at
the full, my dear. That's all.'

' Moon at the full,' indeed, I thought with a
sigh, as he departed, returning an instant afterwards to tell me that he expected a wagon-load
of tubes in the early morning before it was light,
so that Cinders should not see what was coming

into the house, and catch the idea before
Erasmus was too far ahead with his invention to
be overtaken by envy, hatred, and universal
craving for distinction.

Poor Erasmus! I thought. Was he really
going out of his mind, or had that mind at last
struck out some bright original discovery which
should hand him down to fame for Evermore?
There was too much method in his madness for
Erasmus to be very mad, and I hoped for the
Evermore, and waited as patiently as I could,
and took in all kinds of mysterious hampers and
let in mysterious workmen who had been
ordered to come from London surreptitiously,
and who tramped up and down my clean
druggets, carrying upstairs curious-looking
wheels and rods and iron implements—some of
them red hot out of the kitchen fire—and bringing down baskets of broken glass and bits of
fused metal, and even my brother's blue panta-
loons burnt in various portions to a tinder, as if
he had been squibbing somebody and had
materially got the worst of it. Presently there
commenced with much formality the erection of

a steam engine in the back kitchen, and a
summary invasion of the premises of innumerable grimy beings in fustian jackets, and smell-
ing so strongly of grease and iron mould that
Vox Stellarum Villa from that period more
closely resembled a factory than a gentleman's
private and suburban residence.   And finally, a
whole troop of navvies and bricklayers arrived
and bricked round the hole very carefully, and
sat all of a row on the grass-plot one morning
waiting for an enormous boiler, which, after all,
was twenty-four hours behind time, the wagon
which supported it having broken into the main
drainage coming up the hill.

'Erasmus, what does it all mean?   Will you
not confide in me?' I asked at length.

'Anon, anon, child,' he replied, once more;
'we are getting on famously.'

'We shall be ruined with the expense of all
this.'

'We shall be the richest people in the world if
we sell the invention,' he replied.

'Ah! inventors always run away with a foolish
notion of that sort,' I said, acrimoniously; 'the
house is a complete wreck.'

' A complete wreck, Selina ?' he repeated.

' Alas, yes !'

' Then we can't do any further harm by taking down part of the staircase wall. And the flooring will have to come up here and there for the wires,' he said, thoughtfully.

' What wires ?'

' We are running wires from the engine to my study. That's a necessity, because—but you'll tell that Cinders.'

' Ah ! you distrust me, Erasmus.'

' Yes, I do—very much,' he replied, absently, as he walked upstairs carefully counting the steps, or else deep in some new calculation which my presence disturbed.

Time stole on, the dry winter dissolved slowly in the soft arms of spring, and the big boiler was a fact accomplished in the back-garden, and so was the boiler-house, and there were wires all over the establishment, and all leading into the top room where Erasmus worked on in the cause of science and human progress.

At last, towards Christmas time, he came down one evening, very pale and with his grey hair perfectly on end, sat before the fire with his knees resting on the top bars, and said, in a sepulchral voice,

'Selina, it will be done to-morrow.'

'Done! The discovery will be done?'

'Or done for. A great success or a mighty failure—the Lord knows which. But I think,' he added, with a shriek, as he took his knees off the front bars, 'that there is not a doubt of triumph. And then—and then a monument to Erasmus Pascal Stonehouse!'

'You—you—don't mean in a cemetery?' I exclaimed.

'Foolish, babbling trifler—no!' he said, angrily: then he ate a very hearty supper, thoroughly enjoyed it for once, and had seven distinct nightmares, he told me afterwards, before the milkman rang in the morning.

And the morrow came, and with it a big, broad-chested, broad-whiskered, bandy-legged man, in a pilot jacket and a moleskin waistcoat and trousers, whom I hoped I had seen the last of four weeks ago, as he was fond of beer and paid

attentions to the cook. He had assisted in the
erection of the steam-engine and boiler, and had
been altogether very busy and officious, and not
too civil either. He was a man I had particularly disliked, and to whom I had expressed my
mind very clearly once or twice, without in any
way disturbing his.

'Selina, my dear, I think you have seen Mr.
Tomkins before,' Erasmus said to me, by way of
introduction.

'Oh, yes! I have had that pleasure,' I answered, severely.

'Mr. Tomkins is our chief engineer; he will
have entire control of the steam engine, and for
a few weeks, probably, be as one of the family
with us.'

'Oh, dear! indeed,' I ejaculated.

'That is the position, Selina.'

'And whatever'—I began, when Mr. Tomkins had gone downstairs, but Erasmus interrupted me.

'Hush! not a word against Mr. Tomkins,' he
exclaimed. 'My future fame is in his hands.

An over-pressure of steam, an undue allowance of cold water, and everything may be shattered in an instant.'

' Great heaven !' I exclaimed. ' And the insurance ?'

' Every hope may be shattered—I mean every bright dream of the fame for which I have panted and struggled and striven. Where's Cinders ?'

' I don't know where Mr. Cinders is. He has not looked in during the last week,' I replied.

' I had an idea yesterday that he was boring a hole through the party wall on purpose to see what I was about. There was a peculiar grinding sound all day in the next house,' he said.

He had had the painters in, and they were rubbing down the walls preparatory to ' flatting,' I learned afterwards.

' He would never act so shabbily,' I said.

' A good fellow, Cinders, and full of humour,' my brother remarked ; ' but he would certainly die of jealousy if I achieved my fair share of distinction in the world.'

' Genius is prone to jealousy,' I remarked.

'And so is mediocrity, Selina, and ignorance,
and everything else. But there, Tomkins has
begun,' he exclaimed, executing an insane leap
in the air in his excitement, 'I must go to him
at once. The first step depends upon Tomkins.
As for Cinders, he may come to-night, and I shall
be delighted to snap my fingers in his face, in
everybody's face—in the face of the whole
world.'

He ran downstairs to the steam-engine, where
he remained till late in the afternoon, occasionally varying the monotony by running upstairs
three steps at a time to see the effect in his
laboratory, wherein he never failed to lock himself, lest Tomkins should follow him.

I dined alone with Mr. Tomkins that day—
Erasmus altering his mind about having any
dinner at the last moment, and sending me word
that he would take it later on. His heart was
too full, his brain too busy, and he could not
come, he said.

'I hope it's all right with the old gentleman,
ma'am,' said Mr. Tomkins, despondently, 'but
he's in a sad way, to be sure.'

'Of course it's "all right,"' I replied, though I was in a little doubt myself.

'He won't let me have anything to do with the upstairs business,' Mr. Tomkins remarked—'nobody knows what he's doing there, he thinks; but, Lor' bless yer, it's easy to make a guess.'

'Is it?' I asked, anxiously.

'You see, there's been too many hands over this business; and, though I must say the old bloke——'

'Sir!'

'The old gentleman—I beg your pardon, ma'am, for the remark,' he said—'has been blessed artful; but there's no keeping everything quite dark in this world! Me and my mates have talked it over a bit, and, though we haven't been able to make head or tail out of what he's up to, still the general hidea is he's as mad as a March hare upon it.'

'Well—but—but what is he mad upon?'

'A telescope, ma'am.'

'A telescope!'

'Yes; that's it. It's been sticking out of

window the last half-hour. He's a-going to begin, I'm sure.'

'But what is a steam-engine and all these wires to do with a telescope, Mr. Tomkins?'

'Ah! there you gets the best of me, old lady.'

Mr. Tomkins went downstairs to his engine again, and began carrying on a conversation with Erasmus through a gutta-percha tube, which leaked a great deal, for we could hear them all over the house shouting instructions to each other, and a most dreadful uproar they created between them.

Presently Erasmus, in his full-dress suit, entered the room to my profound astonishment.

'Selina,' he said, very solemnly, 'the time has come at last. The great epoch in my career has dawned, and I have dressed to do honour to the occasion.'

'Ye—es. I see.'

'Send Mary to Professor Cinders with my compliments,' he said, 'and will he step round for a few minutes to inspect the great invention? This is an inauguration night.'

The message was despatched to our scientific

neighbour, who sent word in return that he was playing a game at chess with Herr von Flyfischer from Stuttgart, and could not possibly attend.

My brother despatched a second missive. 'Bring Herr von Flyfischer,' was the purport of the epistle, to which the answer was returned that when the contest was concluded Professor Cinders and Herr von Flyfischer would be pleased to drop in for a few minutes.

'As if the matter were of no consequence,' said my brother, irritably; 'as if this night did not herald a complete revolution of everything.'

' I hope not, Erasmus.'

' The greater the revolution the more I shall be talked about,' he said ; 'I wonder how long they will be. I am glad Von Flyfischer is next door; a very able man, Selina, and knows more about the pulsation and capillary attraction of frogs than any *savant* in Europe. What a lucky coincidence he should be at Sydenham to-night !'

He sat before the fire in silence for two more minutes, and I suggested his having dinner now. He thought he would try, but he rose in the middle of his soup—in the middle of drinking his soup, to be precise in this matter—and went downstairs to see how the steam-engine was getting on. When he returned, he asked if Cinders and Von Flyfischer had been heard of yet, as though they were missing in some remote region of the earth.

' Of course they have not, Erasmus. Why, it's not ten minutes since they answered your invitation.'

He went on with his dinner for a minute-and-a-half more ; then said :

' What paltry beings we mortals are. It is all jealousy, petty jealousy, Selina, of my success.'

' Is it a success ?'

' Not a doubt of it,' he cried. ' It is finished and complete ! I sit before you—and before this cold and flabby fish—a man perfectly successful.'

' Oh, Erasmus, *are* you sure ?'

' I am quite sure. Though I have not dared to make the last step yet.'

' You haven't looked through it ?' I asked.

'Looked through what?' And he drew himself up very rigidly at once.

'Is it—isn't it a telescope?'

'Selina, you have been playing the spy upon
me,' he said, with a spasm of anguish distorting
his expressive features.

'No—no—I have not,' I replied. 'It was Mr.
Tomkins who told me at dinner to-day that he
could not make head or tail out of what you
were up to, as he coarsely put it.'

'Tomkins is a sharp fellow,' said Erasmus,
'but no one can do me any harm now. No one is
likely to hit on my calculations, or to fasten on
the clue which has led up to a glorious crisis of
my career, Selina. I shall have a name that
will be handed down carefully and reverently
for generations and generations.'

Was he insane? An inflated idea of one's
own importance was a sure sign of insanity, I
had heard, and Erasmus was certainly 'inflating'
that evening.

'Selina, I will tell you everything,' he said,
leaving off his dinner to sit by my side and take
my hand in his for caution's sake, and to prevent

any exhibition of hysterical excitement on my part. 'I am the inventor—the sole inventor—of an Erasmo-Micro-Electro-Telescope.'

The announcement did not come upon me like a thunder-clap, Mr. Tomkins having done his best to bring about an anti-climax.

'And what is an Erasmo-Micro-Electro-Telescope?' I inquired; 'what will it do?'

'It will combine the telescope to an extent—with the microscope to an unlimited extent; it will combine the telescope and the microscope, with a boundless supply of electricity, and—and what do you think it will do?' he asked, cautiously.

'Explode, perhaps,' I suggested, 'and that is what I have been afraid of all along!'

'Selina, this is childish trifling,' he said. 'Listen: it will so increase the telescopic power, and so magnify that power when increased, that the moon, the planets, the nebulæ, the volatile comet, and the stern fixed stars will all be close at hand! Not twenty yards away, relatively speaking—not twenty feet. They will be with us!'

'Good gracious! What shall we do with them?'

'We shall know all about them, and what is in them, their composition, material formation, the manners and customs of the inhabitants, if any, everything will be bared before us. We'— he sprang to his feet, and frightened me with his cry of exultation, 'I can wait no longer. I will take up Tomkins first. I will try the experiment on Tomkins. He shall immediately follow my first glimpse into the mighty revelations of the stars. Tomkins—ho, there!'

And away bounded my brother in search of the engineer, who having turned on full steam, and seen the engine fairly at work, grinding out innumerable quantities of electric force, was wiling away his leisure moments by chasing the cook round the kitchen-table.

'Tomkins,' I heard Erasmus say, very sternly, 'this is unworthy of you. Come upstairs with me.'

'Yes, sir. Certainly.'

'You have been an agent—if a low and grovelling agent—towards my complete success,

Tomkins, and you shall be the second in the world to marvel at the mysteries of the universe. Science lingers by the wayside and plays chess,' he added, very bitterly, and in allusion to Cinders; 'let honest, horny-handed craftedness take precedence of science. It is ready!'

'May I accompany you, Erasmus?' I inquired.

'Not yet. I am afraid,' he confessed, 'I don't know what is to be seen; and it may not be even fit for a lady to see—for who can tell? Come, Tomkins.'

'And should the professor and Von Flyfischer arrive?' I inquired.

'You can show them upstairs after me. I shall be there waiting.'

'And may I come with them?'

'Yes—with them then,' he said, smiling faintly at my pertinacity. 'By that time all will be known.'

He walked slowly upstairs, followed by Tomkins, who was less elated at the prospect dawning before him than one might naturally have supposed he would be. He would have preferred romping with the cook, I honestly believe.

I listened to their ascending footsteps with a bosom palpitating with emotion ; yes, this was the crisis, and fame might be within a hair's-breadth. My brother thought it was.

The footsteps ascended and ascended, and finally were heard creaking about the top landing. I heard the door of the study unlocked, opened and shut, and then an unnatural silence seemed to reign over the premises. So strangely still it all was as I listened nervously for the least sound of joy, the faintest song of triumph from my brother and his subordinate, that the sudden and heavy knocking at the street door which presaged the arrival of the professor and his friend collapsed me with alarm, and brought me into a sitting posture on the mat at the foot of the stairs.

I recovered myself with difficulty. I tottered to the door, waving back the servant.

' I will admit them,' I said.

I opened the door, and Professor Cinders and Herr von Flyfischer—a very stout little man

with enormous spectacles in tortoiseshell rims—
came into the hall, followed by a long-haired
young man with a book under his arm and a felt
hat on the back of his head. This hat he removed when he was introduced to me, and gave it
in an absent manner to the professor to hold
whilst he bowed.

'Our young friend, the poet of the future,
Mr. Greenstrings,' said the professor; 'he has
been staying with me the last week—he is
engaged to my Clara—thank God!' he added, in
a low aside.

'Oh! indeed, but——'

'Erasmus will be glad to see him,' he said;
'and this is my illustrious friend, Herr von Flyfischer—who unfortunately knows not a word of
English, but will be inexpressibly delighted to
make your acquaintance.'

Herr Flyfischer blinked at me through his
spectacles and bowed profoundly, and put his
hand on his capacious chest, and paid me some
profuse compliments in German.

'And where is your dear brother?' said the
professor.

'In his study. We are all to go to him at once.'

'The end has come, then, of the great mystery,' he remarked, a little spitefully.

'The beginning of it,' I answered, enigmatically ; 'will you please to go upstairs now ?'

We went slowly up the stairs, Herr von Fly-fischer as the honoured visitor from Berlin going first, the poet who was engaged to Clara, second, and the professor and myself bringing up the rear.

We were half way up the first flight of stairs when a terrible scream, a prodigious howl of anguish from above, took every particle of breath out of our bodies, and then, with a mad, thunder-ous clatter, Tomkins, with his hair on end, came bounding down the stairs four steps at a time, and bellowing like a bull. He saw us advanc-ing, a compact body of visitors, but did not stop in any way. On the contrary, only screamed the louder.

' Let me get by—let me get out of this. Oh ! Lord preserve us all—oh !——'

And then he had reached Von Flyfischer, or

had hurled his form at him, or something equally
terrible, for I remembered no more, excepting
a strong German oath which sounded exactly
like English, and then life was a perfect blank
with me, and the professor, and the poet, and
Herr von Flyfischer, all in one dreadful heap at
the bottom of the stairs, and with Tomkins on
the top of the heap, kicking and shouting furi-
ously, finally kicking himself free, darting out
of the front-door, and, with a wail of anguish,
tearing down the street bareheaded, and with
his arms swinging wildly to and fro, as Solomon
Eagle might have done in the days of the Great
Plague.

We gathered ourselves together slowly, Herr
von Flyfischer, with the left eye of his spectacles
crushed into a star pattern, and his nose bleeding slightly above the bridge, assisting me to
rise.

'It has exploded, then?' I murmured.

'We will see,' said Professor Cinders. 'It is
most remarkable, certainly.' And, having recovered from a sense of bewilderment at the
extraordinary behaviour of Tomkins, and being

beset by the idea that something *was* happening in the study, which he should miss if he were not quick, he took to his heels up the stairs at a pace only to be equalled by the rate at which Tomkins had come down them. Herr von Flyfischer, seeing this, set off after him at once, and, asking the poet, who was rubbing his knees in a corner, to be kind enough to shut the street-door for me before he followed, I made all the haste I could myself, lest my brother should need protection from these rival scientists.

And what a scene met us in that study in which Erasmus Pascal had immured himself for so many weeks and months! In a corner of the room, with a large pair of scissors in his hands, and sitting on the floor, with his mouth open more widely than I had ever seen it yet, there sat Erasmus—just as if he were being examined by an imaginary doctor for a quinsy —helpless, prostrate, breathless, with his eyes twice their natural size, and with the same terrified expression upon his countenance which I had witnessed upon Tomkins's before he had knocked me down.

And the room ? A chaotic mass of scientific implements of all kinds was scattered everywhere, as though my brother and Tomkins had been throwing them at each other, or dancing a wild jig amongst them ; whilst at the open window stood a huge telescope on a tripod-stand, with strange wheels and cogs arranged at what I may unscientifically term the butt-end —for the want of a better expression at the moment—and with wires trailing from the telescope and disappearing into Leyden jars, and coming out of Leyden jars again, and making for a box in the corner, and trailing once more from the box a few inches from the floor and disappearing down a tube, which, no doubt, was connected with the steam-engine that had been erected in the back kitchen.

All this I observed at a later period. My only thought now was for Erasmus, the picture of a perfect idiot, cowering and gibbering, and, to a casual observer, making frightfully offensive grimaces at Herr von Flyfischer.

'Erasmus, my dear Erasmus, what has happened?' flinging myself beside him, throwing my arms round his neck impulsively, and running the points of the scissors he was holding through the stomacher of my best black silk; but being mercifully spared from injury by a staybone. 'Tell me what has happened. I am Selina—don't you know me?'

'Don't know any Selinas,' he murmured. 'What planet do you belong to?'

'I am your sister—your only sister, dear.'

'No—no—impossible. No wings,' he said, despondently—'only one head too. Good gracious, only one head, poor thing!'

'He's raving mad—he's gone,' said the professor. 'Whatever is he doing with those scissors? He'll hurt somebody presently.'

'He has hurt me already,' I said, for, though not wounded, the jar had been tremendous.

'No—no—I'm not mad,' cried my brother; 'don't think that, please. That's all nonsense. I am only a bit confused. I shall be better in a year or two. What's a year?'

'Three hundred and sixty-five days, six hours

nearly, sir,' answered the poet, like a man responding to a conundrum.

'Who's that?' asked Erasmus.

'Mr. Greenstrings, my future son-in-law,' said Cinders. 'A rising poet, Stonehouse.'

'Where's his——'

'Where's his what?' I asked, breathlessly, as Erasmus seemed coming to himself slowly.

'Where's his phosphorescence? Why doesn't he shine? The Lord have mercy upon him, why doesn't he shine like all the rest of them?'

'Yes, he's clean gone,' said the professor. 'It's turned his brain, whatever it is. I should send round to the station for a hansom, and take him off to an asylum at once. I don't think there's any time to be lost, Miss Stonehouse.'

'I'm perfectly sane, thank you,' said my brother, quite chirpily. 'Take the hansom yourself, you bald-headed old egotist!'

'Well, of all—Stonehouse, do you know who I am?' said the professor.

'You're Cinders, the man who lives next door —at least, you look like him; but you are marvellously changed, and as tailless as a guinea-pig.'

' Completely wrecked !' said Cinders, holding up his hands in pity for me. ' Miss Selina, I fear the little brains he ever had are completely shattered.'

' Let me bleed him,' said Von Flyfischer, very promptly, to the professor; and though he spoke in German, I perfectly understood him when he produced a pocket-lancet.

' You shall not shed a drop of his blood !' I shrieked forth. ' Erasmus, pray collect yourself. What are you sitting on the floor for ?'

' I am sitting here in astonishment, Selina !'— (he knew me—he was coming to himself)—' in perfect bewilderment, horror, and admiration ! I did not anticipate—I should not have thought —no living, breathing being on the surface of the earth could have possibly imagined—it's beyond human conjecture—it's too much alto-gether—it's altogether too much—and coming with a rush in this manner, and to be suddenly introduced into an entirely new state of things —it's—it's overwhelming ! That's all !' And he shut his eyes, as if the mental prospects were too much for him now.

'What can it be?' ejaculated the professor. 'Is it possible that this is a plagiarism, Stonehouse?' he asked sternly of my brother.

'My own invention, entirely,' gasped forth Erasmus, feebly.

'Two years ago I lectured on the sidereal system in this very room to a select but learned audience; we had models of the system in active revolution—Dutch cheeses coated with luminous paint, and all going at once: we——'

'It's my own discovery,' murmured Erasmus; 'I have brought the stars to earth; I have been in the interior of Jupiter; and—oh! you can never imagine anything so——Will anybody oblige me with a glass of water?'

Some one—the poet it was, I think, who came in so handily on this occasion—ran downstairs and got the water-bottle off the sideboard in the dining-room.

'What is that?' asked the professor, pointing to the telescope.

'It's my Erasmo-Micro-Electro-Telescope.

It's perfect—it's too perfect. I'll never undertake the responsibility of upsetting the whole world—I can't—I won't !'

' Whatever can it be that——'

The professor walked towards the telescope on tiptoe ; he was stooping to peer through the eyeglass, when Erasmus curdled the blood in all our bodies again by the wildest of screams.

' Don't, Cinders, don't ! Your brain is *not* strong enough. We shall all be in asylums if this continues. Cinders, pray *don't !*'

Professor Cinders bestowed on poor Erasmus a look of utter scorn.

' You have asked me here as a guest,' he said, coldly but cuttingly ; ' you have asked my learned friend, Von Flyfischer ; I have taken the liberty of bringing a young gentleman of high ability, who is engaged to my eldest daughter, Clara, and we cannot be made the dupes of deception, or the victims on your part of a practical joke.'

' I never made a joke in my life,' said Erasmus, who was too weak to argue or resent reproach.

'And,' continued the professor, for whom I shall never entertain again one atom's worth of respect, 'if your brains have stood the test of this marvellous discovery, I flatter myself that I shall be able to survive.'

He advanced again, and Erasmus passed the scissors to me.

'Save him,' he murmured, in a husky whisper. 'It must be done. Sever the connection.'

'I dare not attack him, Erasmus. I——'

'Cut that wire; that's all. Cut it, cut it!'

I understood now; and as the professor turned the broadest portion of his frame towards us, and stooped slowly and a little nervously towards the marvellous proof of Erasmus's great genius, I snipped in half the copper wire at my side in solemn silence, and Erasmus laid his head upon my shoulder, and, with a long quivering sigh of relief, went off like a babe into a most refreshing slumber.

Meanwhile, the professor had applied his left eye to the telescope, then his right eye, had drawn forth his pocket-handkerchief, breathed on the glass, and polished it, had stooped again .

and tried his left eye and his right once more, had finally stood up and faced us with an expression absolutely withering.

'I can't see a single thing. Not a single thing *is* to be seen,' he affirmed. 'This is the freak of a lunatic.'

'We—we had better run round for the hansom,' murmured the poet.

'Hush!' I exclaimed, 'not so much noise now; he sleeps.'

'Let him sleep, and be blowed,' cried the professor, devoid, in his impotent rage, of the commonest decencies of civilised life; 'if he has taken to play the fool and the mountebank, this is the last time he will play it on me, or on any friend of mine. Come, Von Flyfischer, come, Greenstrings; it's no use your trying to see anything through that thing'—they had taken it in turns now to inspect,—'it's a dummy, or he has bunged up the other end. He was anxious to make fools of us, and he has made fools of us, and I wish him joy of his success.'

Then away marched the professor, and the professor's friend, and the professor's future son-

in-law, and I was left in a corner of the laboratory, with my brother's head pillowed on my
heaving chest, where it remained till I thought
that I should die of cramp.

He came to himself in the middle of the night
—he was aroused by the boiler exploding in
the back garden, I may observe, for the steam-
engine, which had been going on madly by
itself downstairs, had been utterly forgotten—
opened his eyes and surveyed me very sadly.

'Selina Stonehouse,' he said, 'they have all
gone, then.'

'Yes, they have all gone.'

'You have saved them, but none the less it
was a marvellous discovery.'

He rose, and I rose with him, every bone
aching most dreadfully.

'I think I should like some supper now,' he
said. 'I cannot understand why I am so
frightfully hungry.'

'Thank Heaven, you are your noble self
again,' I ejaculated.

'I always was,' he answered back; 'but the
invention was too much for me—too much for

anybody. The responsibility is not with me to alter every human aspiration and upset every science. Let it perish. Here goes!'

And in one moment he had tilted the big telescope out of the window, whence it went crashing through the glass roof of the conservatory—once again and for the last time bringing Professor Cinders upon the scene, who leaned half out of his own back window with his night-cap on.

'What the devil is it now?' he cried; 'has he thrown himself out? Has he committed suicide?'

'No, it's only the telescope.'

'Oh, that's a pity.'

And then the window was slammed down.

That is my story. Erasmus Pascal Stonehouse invented nothing more. I do not think he has been the same man since, and certainly he is a little more absent, and studies not at all. Sometimes he sighs, as though he regrets the sacrifice of his great invention; but he always maintains it was too much of a discovery. And I believe him.

Tomkins, the engineer, never ceased running, I have heard, till he reached Liverpool, where he took steamer for New York, and has not been heard of since. He left a wife and seven children to the care of Camberwell parish, which is still advertising for his whereabouts, and will be extremely obliged to any lady or gentleman who can favour it with any authentic particulars respecting him.

ANOTHER MAN'S WIFE.

ANOTHER MAN'S WIFE.

TEN years ago I ran away with Trafford's wife.
That is the plainest way of putting it. I set it
down here just as if I were not writing of myself, just as if, God help me, it was not possible
I could have been at any time of my career so
weak, so desperate, and so despicable a villain.

So weak—because the woman was pretty and
romantic, and thought she loved me until it was
too late to love anybody else. *So desperate*—
because mine was a name looked up to ; I was
one in whom people believed, and I was clever
enough in my way to have made my mark, to
be talked of, to be flattered. What I was does
not matter to the purport of this confession—

what I came to does, and in its proper place
will be related here. *So despicable*—because the
woman's husband was a good man, and I hardened him to stone; a happy, trustful man, and
I wrecked his happiness and trust; a father, and
I took away the mother of his children.

That is why I said just now, God help me. I
have said of late days, God forgive me, too;
only of late days this is, and for a reason to be
presently explained, and I say it with all the
heart and soul and strength left in me.

I could preach of 'extenuating circumstances'
if I were sure of a sympathetic audience, but I
should shriek at my own excuses afterwards,
shriek with a mocking horror, as the fiends
shriek. I was a sentimentalist and a fool; if I
have one excuse that is worth recording it is
that I loved the woman—that I believed her
life would be brighter with me than with him,
and that I resolved all my life to try to make it
so. There was no thought of a fleeting passion,
of a setting her aside, of a lower depth for her, of
the old story of the streets; it was the sacrifice
of my life and honour to her life and shame, and

in its early days it was set down to romance, to
the 'affinities,' to a something which two mis-
guided souls, proceeding rashly their own way,
could afford to call their fate.

All a delusion, all very common-place, and
miserable, and cruel, and, my God! the waking
to the fact that it was so!—the stern truth that
name and fame, and good men's thoughts of us,
had wholly passed from our sphere, and we were,
even in our own hearts, accursed things.

If I could have been—if she could have been
—as callous as are some folk ; if we could have
forgotten the past wherein people thought so
well of us, if the present could have been everything without a thought of what had been, or
of what might come to us, of the horror and the
disgrace to grow upon us when the glamour of
the sin had vanished, and we were simply every-
day sinners, without a single excuse! To me
the life has been ever unbearable, and yet I have
borne it. To her it has been a reproach which
she has been unable to hide from me, a sting
which has struck into her heart and poisoned its
life current, and turned her brain at times. And

we each disguised from the other for a while
what a mockery our lives together were, what
an ordeal of mental anguish, what a damnable
and awful failure.

If she *had* been heartless, if she could have
become so by degrees; if the days, and months,
and years passing by with us could have rendered us as callous as sin *can* make people, we
could have borne life with a greater patience,
and almost with a light heart. But this is not
the story of our lives together, or why I let the
daylight in upon it now.

There was no romance left between us; we
had chosen our lot, but we despised it. We
were verily ashamed, but there was no return to
goodness. The great gates were shut, and we
did not pray for them to open, and let us back
to our old lives, our old homes, our old self-
respect, and the loves of those whom we still
loved and dared not say a word concerning.
We were silent tortures to ourselves.

We had sacrificed our lives, but there was no
confidence in the new estate; on the contrary,
there was complete restraint. The curse of a

strong imagination was always upon us, and made us worse. We did not believe in each other; we wondered at each other's thoughts, and what regrets, repinings, remorse, were commingled with them. Sometimes I found her in tears, in an utter prostration of grief, and she would not tell me why she wept, and why it was beyond my power to console her. I have been always left to wonder what it was that would suddenly crush and abase her, and yet to know that it was Trafford she was thinking of, and of Trafford's children—not hers, for she had abandoned them!—who rose up like accusing angels, and looked towards her, and even talked of her as 'dear mamma who was dead,' and whom she could never take again to her heart.

And I? I had repented long ago. My life was one curse of helplessness. There was a vague sense of duty to this victim, a feeling that I must atone for wrecking her life, by trying to make it endurable to her, and the awful consciousness that I was not succeeding, that I could not render it anything but one profitless series of reproaches, which were not spoken to me, but which every action and every look betrayed.

I could have reproached *her*, had I had the cruel courage to do so, but in all our life together I did not say a word. I could have told her of her own folly, of her great and little vanities, her recklessness, her resentments, her futile reasonings with the clear-headed, strong-hearted surgeon who had married her five years ago, and would have had her as good and staid and homelike as were other wives about his sphere. I could have scoffed at her desire for absolute admiration and power, her foolish resistance to control, the self-will which at last cast her into my arms and away from the better man's. I knew her character—I could read it like a book. I could influence it for good or harm, and I sank my own identity to make her career with me the record of her own self-satisfaction. It was her own way absolutely —her own life, not mine—but no roses ever strewed the path along which we went together, only the dust and ashes which grew deeper and thicker with every step we took away from right.

Ten years afterwards it might have been thought that we had settled down, but we never had. She was thirty-five years of age then, and as pretty and graceful a woman as she had ever been; the only change in her was in the depth of grave, strange thought which, in repose, her features always showed. That long look ahead was very sad to watch, and one need not wonder of what she was thinking, or of the figures in the distance that flitted before her yearning gaze. And she did not know herself how long she would look thus, or how completely she had drifted from the life about her, and from the home that had never seemed to be hers. On the contrary, she would reproach me with my long brooding fits, my forgetfulness of *her*, and there would come the terrible fear that *will* come to women like her, that I had grown weary of it all, and would be quit of it soon, without much thought for her. There were times when she would tell me this as the deep conviction which she had, and I had to deny its truth to keep her sane, knowing in my heart how true it was, and that the life was one which I continually deplored. And yet there had never come to me a resolution to escape it—mine had been a career deliberately adopted, and it must go on to the end. It could not be altered without my being to the world a greater villain than I was already. I had repented, but no man or woman would have believed in such a repentance as mine; 'he has thrown her off,' would have been the outcry against me. I had acted like a hound from the beginning to the end, and it was like me. What else could have been expected? Poor woman!

We had lost sight of Trafford all these ten years. We had tried to forget him; we had been abroad, moving from place to place; we had left him to his London practice in a western suburb of London, so far as we knew, and he had not endeavoured in any way to find us out. He had let us go from his sight. He had not sought to obtain a divorce, for he had not thought of taking to himself a second wife, and he was content with the two children—one boy, one girl—which she had left with him. We did not even know that he had become famous in those ten wasted years of ours, and that men spoke of him with admiration and with gratitude, the gift of healing being a God's gift with him which had worked great ends. There were stories of his goodness as well of his eccentricity, but we had not heard of them then; of his generosity, of his bad temper, of his power, of his pride, as there are stories, false and strange, of all men who rise above the level of their fellows. It was not till we were back again in London, tired out with many cities, that I came across his name in the newspapers, found that it was not easy to escape the name which cropped up in every important case connected with the court or the nobility. People sick unto death seemed to cry aloud for Sir Edward Trafford; he had been plain Ned Trafford when I stole his wife away, a man of strong opinions and firm will, but one who I had never thought would rise to honours such as he had gained.

I tried at first to keep the newspapers from

her, but she was fond of news. The theatrical
world interested her, the concert world, the
world of art and literature, and she would have
guessed my motive had I made any marked
effort to conceal news from her. She must
have seen his name very frequently at last, but
she never alluded to it; in London she grew
more restless and excited, and was even strange
at times and gave me great concern, as for a
new trouble that might be advancing. We
were out a great deal; the theatre and concert-
room were our distractions; we were not fond
of home, we were strangely glad to escape it.
It was not pleasant to sit facing each other for
long hours, and to be uncertain what thoughts
were troubling us—even if one might not despise the other in that heart of hearts which was
under lock and key. We had no society; we
were to have been 'all in all,' and we still
shrank from those friends we might have had,
or the few honest, trusting folk who would have
believed in 'the respectabilities' about our
darkened world, and called us friends of theirs.
We were above deceiving them: we accepted

our position and lived very staidly; we would have no new friends, and we had set ourselves apart from all the old.

Now and then, strange accidents occurred and unlooked-for meetings. The world is full of them, and we could not escape them. Ten years had not swept us out of those terrible memories for faces and incidents which some people have. I need not speak of them more; they were part of our trials which there was no eluding, they were part of our contract.

It had often occurred to me that I should have been glad to meet a man like myself, of my thoughts and character, some one who had done as I had done, and to whom I could talk and reason—and, if it were so, confess. What a hundred questions I could have asked *him!*— whether his life's sin had been worth an hour of his better life? whether he had lived down remorse, or if remorse had made his life a hell? And when such a man by chance confronted me, some one whom I knew by evil repute to be a man like me—as bad as I was!—strange feeling that it was, I could shrink from him as

from one lost beyond redemption, and whose
career had been a scandal and a gross affront
to me! I was a sentimentalist, I have said
already. The reader of these lines will not understand me without knowing of my weakness.
I could not make the best of my position; it was
beyond me.

I was thirty-seven years of age and a rich
man comparatively, when I came back to London with her. I was in the prime of life, when
life should have been at its best, and yet I
could envy the workman with his child strolling
in the public park through which I dashed on
horseback. I would have changed places with
him had the chance been offered me and at the
price of my forgetfulness. If I could have only
forgotten! If I could have hardened like steel,
and been like other men! If she had been
happy, very happy, say moderately happy, and
kept me from thinking desperately—if in her own
strange sadness there was not ever a lost soul's
whisper to me—' This is your work! without
you I should have been an honest woman at
peace with God, at peace with myself!'

One thing I had been spared hitherto in this miserable association—the curse which comes to most men who have acted after my fashion—jealousy. In no instance during those ten years had she raised my mistrust; in no instance had I seen in her that instinct to attract, to encourage, to flatter other men, which is part of a weak woman's character, and which had led her from her husband's side to mine. The first fault had been the great fault, and she was faithful to me—terribly faithful! Shall I own that there were times when I regretted this—when it crossed my mind that there might have been an excuse to close the sin of it, with a blacker sin for her; that it would be even a natural sequel to a commonplace history, and so an end to it, and a retracing of my weary steps along the way I had come?

When we were in London again the jealousy came at last, and I was amazed at the strength and passion of it—at its bewildering effects upon me. She became more eccentric in her manner, a woman with a mystery, a woman who would not explain. There were days when I returned home to find she had deserted it, and soon the various excuses offered for her absence aroused my suspicions and did not appear to be the truth. Which they were not. Which presently I proved to be lies, but such lies as disarmed my jealousy and filled me with a new despair.

She had discovered her children. She had found out her husband's residence in a West-end square, and she had planned and plotted to see them, even to speak to them with all the earnestness and passion of a woman at bay.

'Why did you not tell me?' I asked, when the secret came out at last, 'why hide it all from me?'

'You would have been angry.'

'No.'

'And I could *not* keep away. For the soul of me, Ernest, I could not keep away. I wanted to see them, oh, so badly.'

'It can do no good.'

'I know that.'

'It may do a deal of harm.'

'It may,' she assented.

'You have not told them who you are?'

'Oh, no, God forbid that! I have only asked
them a direction in the street, just to hear the
sound of their voices, just to look at them a little
closer and be sure that they are my own boy
and girl. Don't you understand me?' she screamed, 'won't you understand me?'

'Yes, yes, I understand,' was my reply; 'but
this will drive you mad.'

'It may.'

'It is too late in the day for this exaggerated
sentiment,' I added, even harshly; 'had you
loved your children more, you would not have
gone away from them.'

'That's true,' she answered, gloomily; 'I own
it. I was selfish. I did not think of them at
first. I thought only of you then. I——'

'Oh, Eva, forgive me. I did not mean to cast
that dart at you.'

'It is all true,' she said; 'I did not think of
them a great deal, and I—I knew they would
be happy with their father, and well cared for
and loved. He was always very fond of children,
a just, good, hard man,' she added, thoughtfully,
'and very fond of children, very.'

'You see, all this has brought fresh misery to
you; rendered you wholly unhappy and restless.
What is the use of it?' I asked.

'I don't know,' was the helpless answer, and
she wrung her hands together for an instant; 'I
am not trying to see the use of it, the good of it.
How should I know what is good? I don't
even understand why it should come to me after
all these years to find them out, to yearn for one
look of their bright young faces, as one like me
might yearn to look at heaven just for once—
but it has come, and they *are* my boy and girl.
Whatever I am—whatever I have been—they
are mine. Don't you see that? Don't you see
I can't help all this? I can't! I can't!'

Her grief, her self-abandonment was so great
that I could only attempt to soothe it, implore
her to be calm, to be reasonable, to forget my
harshness, to exercise some sort of self-restraint,
and then the calm followed—that dread calm
which was very like despair.

I did not set an interdict on her movements;
I did not inquire again where she had been; I
had to let things take their course and remain in

ignorance as to which way they were tending.
I seemed to expect a catastrophe—to be waiting
for it—to be wondering how long it would be.
And yet I was not wholly passive, I was making
arrangements to go abroad again, to be quit of
England, this time, for ever.

When the time came to tell her, she shook her
head sadly.

'I cannot go,' she answered.

'I have made all preparations.'

'You will kill me, if you take me from
England any more,' she said; 'but, if you insist,
I must die.'

I did not answer. I resolved to speak of it
again to-morrow, when she was less excitable,
when she had grown more accustomed to the
news. I had surprised and shocked her. I was
not a wise man. I did nothing that was
right.

And, on the morrow, the catastrophe for which
I had waited had come, and there was no talking or reasoning with her again. It had come
to myself—to me who was unprepared for it,
who had not looked for it in my own direction,

had not dreamed the hand of fate could strike so heavily.

My horse had taken fright, and I had been thrown. It was a terrible accident, and they picked me up, as they thought, for dead. I was carried to the nearest hospital, in one of the wards of which I found myself days afterwards, lying like a child, speechless, nerveless, with not even the strength to turn my head. Strange faces came and looked at me for an instant and then vanished in a mist that grew about them; voices very far away sounded meaninglessly in my ears, where there was always the rushing of a sea and the breaking of its waves in thunderous booms upon the beach. I must be at sea, I mused, when the first thought came back to me.

There was no power to move, I was like a man chained down. At that time I did not know what had happened, whether I was not in a dream or trance; everything about and around me belonged so completely to the unknown, and it was so full of clouds, into which I was always vanishing, sometimes very slowly, at other times with a celerity that was like being hurled into an unknown depth and then forgotten.

A woman's face, looking intently into mine, was the first thing I recollected as part of waking life. A strange, kind face, and yet I whispered 'Eva,' wonderingly, as at a change in her, for which I was unprepared, and yet I was not wholly surprised.

'Ah! I am not Eva,' said my nurse, smiling.

'Then——'

'Hush. You must not talk any more. You must wait.'

I remembered that injunction, and obeyed her. I read the meaning in her clear, bright face, and said no more. The doctors came and looked at me, and I would have spoken to one of them, but he shook his head, and lightly touched his lips with his fingers before he turned to those about him.

'He's conscious,' one said.

'Marvellous!' ejaculated a little man, with dark spectacles.

'Will he pull through? Is it possible?' asked another.

'Hardly.'

Then they passed on down the ward, and I lay and thought they were talking of somebody else, and faintly wondered where they had come from, and why they all had looked at me, till I floated away once more into forgetfulness.

By-and-by—a day afterwards, I was told it was—I became more conscious of surrounding objects, animate and inanimate; I knew that I was an inmate of one of the wards of a large London hospital, and that bandages were on my head, that my limbs were in splints, and I was powerless.

'What has happened?' I asked.

The nurse told me in soft whispers and with her cautious eyes upon me all the while. My horse had taken fright and I had been thrown. I had been brought to that hospital, and it was thought I could not recover; it was beyond human skill to save me, it was thought, but I was still alive, and it was hoped that now I was likely to live, with a little extra care and special nursing.

'Thank Heaven!' I answered.

Life had not appeared to be of much value to me before my accident ; I had contemplated the easiest means of quitting it once or twice ; but, strangely, it was of great value to me now.

'You have Sir Edward Trafford to thank for your life,' said the nurse.

'Sir Edward Trafford?'

'No one else could have succeeded with the operation.'

It was a complicated case of trepanning that had been the most difficult part of the matter, one that Sir Edward had carried out on a new principle which was to still further enhance his fame in the world. I was amazed, discomfited, cast down. The nurse saw the change in me, and called out for further assistance. I remembered nothing more that day.

My return to consciousness, to the state of a reflective being, was marked by what they thought was a stern reserve, an odd manner altogether. I might be going mad—it was one of the results which they feared—and they were very observant. There seemed some one al-

ways flitting near me, watching me; I had
hardly the time to think for myself, to wonder
what was to be done and said after all this.

I was getting stronger of speech: I could
think; and I was growing beset by two terrible
fears: what had become of Eva? when would
Sir Edward Trafford come and look down upon
me lying there as the other doctors looked?

'Has he been here?' I asked.

'Sir Edward?'

'Yes.'

'He came every day for the first week. You
were his case—you are his case,' said the nurse.

'Will he come again?'

'Yes, to be sure. He is away just now, but
you are in good hands. You must not worry
about that. You *are* getting better. Sir Edward will be back in a few days.'

She talked very rapidly, and I could not in-
terrupt her. When she had done, I said aloud
—and it seemed impossible to help saying,—

'I do not wish to see him.'

The nurse looked surprised.

'Am I compelled?' I asked.

'I don't see how you can help it,' she said, regarding me with new interest; 'you are Sir Edward's case, I have told you.'

'Yes.'

After a pause, she said,

'Why don't you wish to see him?'

I was silent. I saw that I had acted wrongly if I wished to keep my secret. I replied to her at last,

'I don't know—I can't tell.'

'I should think not,' she said, brusquely, as she walked away.

Late in the day one of the surgeons came to me, talked to me, congratulated me on my better state.

'Am I out of danger?' I asked, anxiously.

'Well, not absolutely out of danger. You must be careful, of course.'

'Could I not leave here—be carried home—at any cost. Money is no object to me, and I would be so glad to get away!' I urged.

'It is quite impossible.'

'To-morrow, or the next day?'

'Not for many days. You must be resigned

Q 2

to this, my good fellow. There is no jumping
back to your old self at a bound.'

He laid his hand kindly on my shoulder and
said,

'You must be thankful for coming back to
the world at all. You must be patient—it is
your one chance.'

'I cannot be patient here.'

'You must try, Mr. Elwin.'

I flinched at the mention of my name. I
felt like a man stabbed, like a man betrayed. I had hoped they did not know me
at this hospital; that I was one of many, and
unrecognised: that there had been no clue to
my identity. I knew now that my card-case
had not been in my pocket; that I had no
letters with my address upon them, and I fancied it had been no one's particular business to
trace and track me out. My linen was only
marked with my initials, and I had hugged
myself with the conviction that I was not
known, and that by care and a sacrifice of
my feelings I might pass unknown from the
hospital.

From the moment of the mention of Trafford's name, I had resolved to be as silent as the grave —to ask no question as to Eva—to send no message to her—to leave her even in the agony of doubt as to what had become of me. Better that, better anything, than that I should be known as Ernest Elwin, the man who, ten years ago, ran away with Trafford's wife.

Sir Edward Trafford had not recognised me, I was certain—the poor, crushed wretch, bleeding and dust-begrimed, was, in the confusion of the accident, not likely to be known ; and ten years had made enough change in me, without calamity. And yet this man called me Elwin, as if he knew me very well.

' Why do you say Elwin ?' I asked.

'I don't know,' said the surgeon, carelessly; ' it is Elwin, is it not ?'

He was short-sighted, and he walked to the head of the bed, peered closely at a large card affixed there which stated the nature of my case, my diet, and my treatment, and all particulars for the information of the surgeons and students going to and fro : and my name and number were there also, it was evident.

'You're down here as Elwin—Ernest Elwin. Is it wrong, then?' he asked.

I did not answer: I could have shouted ·Yes!' in my rage and distress, but it would have been a foolish lie. Some one had recognised me, or something had betrayed me, and my long silence had been all in vain. I had not spoken of my home, and no one had cared to ask me concerning it; if there had been anybody whose anxiety I could allay, they thought probably I should have been the first to mention it, of course. But I had been very silent, very grim. It had seemed to me better that Eva should remain in suspense awhile, than that she should come here and possibly meet *him*. The great surprise was over by this time, and it was only a short time longer. Had she known I should not have been allowed to see her yet awhile, she would have called persistently and been discovered. All this, I had had the strength to plan out, to feel the misery of it all,

and yet to feel sure it was the best. And after
all there was my name at the head of the bed,
and the secret I had kept so close exposed to
those who cared to read.

'Is it wrong?' the surgeon asked again.

'It is quite right,' I replied at last. 'But who
put my name up there?'

'I don't know.'

Later in the day I asked the nurse, and she
could not inform me either. It had been a
matter of form—done by one of the students,
she supposed—she could not say.

'Strange!' I muttered, doubtfully.

'I don't recognise the handwriting either,'
she said, looking at the card in her turn, 'it's
not the usual writing. Does it matter?'

'No.'

But I lay and tried to puzzle out the meaning
till I grew very faint and went back a step or
two towards a relapse. When I was well
enough to speak again next day, I asked that
a message might be sent to my home explain-
ing to Eva where I was, and saying that she

must not come to see me; that I must not see
anyone yet—it was Sir Edward Trafford's instructions.

'Say Sir Edward Trafford's,' I pleaded, 'and
ask her to write to me instead, and assure me
she's well.'

In due course the answer came. There were
only a few words, and I had thought she might
have sent me a longer letter.

'I have been already told of your accident,
and have promised for your sake to keep away,'
she wrote. 'I am terribly bewildered. I pray
every night—I, who have not prayed for years—
for your recovery. I am ill.

'Eva.'

She had known all, then; but who was there
in the hospital to inform her of my accident?
Her address was not on the books, and there was
no one to whom my accident was of any extra
interest, save from a scientific or surgical point
of view. Unless—and I tried to think if it
were possible—Sir Edward Trafford had done

all this himself, had recognised me, found out my address, and written to her who had been once his wife. Surely impossible!

The probable return of the great surgeon to town filled me with dismay, and retarded my progress to recovery. What would he say when he saw my name at the head of the bed? What would he think? What would he do?

I owed my life to the man whose home I had shadowed, whose name I had dishonoured, and my life was valueless in his eyes and my own. If I could escape before his return; if I could only get away before he looked down upon me with his great, inquiring, dark eyes! I seemed suddenly to remember his eyes, and how they glistened through the glasses which he had always worn. I grew afraid of them. If I could only steal away! If I could escape him!

Then came the relapse in earnest, born of all this mental struggle of which I could not, dared not speak, and all was chaos to me, from which I emerged at last, weaker than I had ever been. I had come back from delirium—there had been

another operation necessary; I had been carried to the Theatre, and back to my bed,
without my knowledge; there had been a cold,
critical discourse upon my case to the students
who had thronged the operating room to gather
knowledge from my suffering, from the lips
of the great surgeon who so seldom addressed
them now, and only in important cases like my
own.

In the twilight, before there were lights burning in the wards, one day when I was stronger,
I woke from my sleep to find him sitting at my
bedside. The nurse was near him talking in a
low voice, and he was listening attentively.
My heart seemed to stop still when I was sure it
was he.

I was right. I knew him by his eyes. In
all else he was a changed man. He was nine
years Eva's senior, but I had not thought to see
him with hair as white as snow, and with a
hundred fine deep lines about his face. It was
a very stern face, with the thin lips compressed,
as I had always known them; but it was handsome still, for all its gravity and oldness of ex-

pression. A face of intense power, a clever man's face, from which a poor, weak sinner like myself seemed to cower and try to hide away, lest its very looks should blast him.

'This is Sir Edward,' said the nurse.

'I know,' I murmured, hoarsely.

'Leave us,' followed the dry, hard tones of the surgeon, and with a 'Certainly, Sir Edward,' the nurse departed.

Then there was a silence. He looked steadily at me, as I had thought he would look, and I looked away from him down the ward, and along the row of sufferers there.

'Elwin!' he said at last, and I glanced wistfully towards him. I tried to speak, but could not.

'You have had two hard fights for your life,' he said, calmly, and without a quaver of his voice, 'but you are spared, I am glad to say.'

'Glad?' I murmured.

'Yes—very glad.'

I could not reply. Strange hot tears came to my eyes, whose founts had been sealed for years.

'We are always glad when we succeed in a difficult case, and yours has been the most critical that I have ever known,' he continued, in a hard, metallic way, that brought me slowly to myself. 'It is a triumph of surgery to restore you to the world.'

To restore me to his wife! Did he think of that in the midst of his success, I wondered? Or was that a matter which did not concern him in the least now, which was not any part of his thoughts? Yes, he was a hard man; she had always called him hard and unsympathetic; it had been his profession first, and his wife second, and his wife had resented the preference, fretted, complained, and fled.

'He will never miss me,' she had said, 'he will be happier without me.'

Perhaps he had been. Who could tell, looking into that inflexible face, whether he had suffered or not? I was not sure, even, whether he knew me; he spoke so calmly, and regarded me as a patient in whom, on account of the complications of the case, he was more than ordinarily interested. And for no other reason?

'Do you know who I am?' I asked at last, fretful and impatient.

'You must keep cool, sir,' he said politely, but firmly; 'excitement is all we have to fear in you.'

'You do not answer my question, Sir Edward.'

'Why do you ask?'

'I cannot say—I cannot explain,' I replied. 'But I would be very glad to know.'

'Will it ease your mind to know?'

'I think it will.'

'Yes. I knew you directly you were brought into the hospital. I never forget a face,' he said, quietly.

'Why did you not kill me when I was so completely in your power?' I burst forth. 'I deserved it—I——'

He laid his hand upon my arm, and rose from the bedside.

'There, there, that will do,' he said. 'You must recollect a surgeon's pride, his fame, rests on the saving of his patient, not the killing of him.'

'Ah! well, you may kill me presently in a fairer way,' I said. 'I am at your orders, always.'

'Thank you,' he said, drily, 'I know that. And now try to sleep. And a good-night to you, for it is what you need most.'

He walked down the ward somewhat feebly, I thought, for his four-and-forty years, and the nurses rose and curtsied to him as he passed, and the patients watched him with their big, wondering eyes, a giant amongst men, and as he stopped at the far end of the room, before one who was also his especial care, the students pressed closely round him, and hung upon his words.

'A good man, is he not, nurse?' I said to the attendant who had approached my side again.

'I don't know. He is a great man, at all events.'

'Yes.'

'It is an honour to us for him to come now,' she said, 'an honour to you that he should have been so deeply interested in you. Everybody has thought him particularly interested. But

then it's a miracle that you're alive, with a skull
all smashed into the brain as yours has been.
Why,' she added, cheerfully, in order to raise a
smile in me, ' you've no business to be alive at
all. It's against the record.'

' No. I have no business to be alive,' I murmured. ' That is it.'

' Ah! well, go to sleep,' she said, soothingly,
' you'll be more cheerful in the morning.'

Cheerful! In the morning I waited very
anxiously for him. I longed to see him; I had
thought of many things which I should like to
say, and I wished to find the courage, the
strength, to say them, and to thank him for all
his consideration for me. But he came not that
day, nor the next. He was keeping out of my
way now; perhaps he thought his presence disturbed me, and led to an excitement that was
injurious; or, having set me on the road to con-
valescence, there was gone all interest in the
matter, and he left me to men whose time was
not so precious as his own.

I had got well enough to see visitors at last,
but I had begged Eva not to come yet—not to

come at all. And it was for her husband's sake, rather than for hers. I would have spared him. I was beset by a strange, unknown fear of those two meeting, and possibly at my bedside. It was too horrible to contemplate.

She did not come. She took me at my word and left me to myself. And I was greatly relieved. The fear of seeing her was awfully strong upon me—the woman who had shared my life, who had sacrificed her life for me, and to whom I had surrendered my ambitions, my friends, my honourable career—the woman who was my whole life, I did not wish to see. I was afraid of any grief or excitement which she might betray—I was more afraid of her indifference—still more of the thoughts she might have of her husband, and her wish to beg for his forgiveness, and to tell him how bitterly she had repented of the wrong that she had done him.

She did not answer my note, and I was glad of that. There was always in her letters, amidst the kindliness of her nature, the ring of the natural discontent at what she was, the wail sometimes over what she might have been, disguise it as she might by obscure words and phrases. I had been always in dread, in the few times that I had been away from her, what sorrow might be shadowed forth in every missive to myself. In returning to her, I had always wondered what might have happened in my absence, and always, as I approached our home, been, as it were, prepared for something. There was a selfish satisfaction in knowing that she would not come, that there was no letter for me, that I was left in peace, and alone, to get well.

The next time Sir Trafford visited this ward of the hospital, to my astonishment he passed me by. He had paid some extra attention to the patient at the remote end of the ward—a man I did not know even by sight, but of whom I felt jealous!—and then he came slowly along, accompanied by students and one or two surgeons from other hospitals; and, like a king attended by his suite, he passed by me. He did not even glance towards me. I was a man forgotten.

Why I felt this slight so acutely, why I

grieved over it, it is difficult to say. The sick
man is all self; the whole world belongs to him,
and he is the central figure in it. Had he been
the dearest friend of my life I could not have
felt this setting me aside with a deeper grief.
I could imagine in my weakness that he had
done me a cruel wrong to ignore my existence
in this way. He had brought me to life again,
but it was the fable of Frankenstein: he did
not love the monster for all the life that he had
given him. I was *his* monster, and he shunned
me. Might he not even regret this in his heart,
—that he had recreated me to work more evil,
to go on as I had begun, to feel that it was
my duty to sin on, bending to man's law and
his code of honour, for the sake of the
woman!

If Trafford would only speak to me, if he
would sit down by my bedside and let me
speak, if he would only come again, so that I
might just see him and look my gratitude, I
thought at last. But days went by and weeks,
and I was able to get up, able in a few days
more, they told me, to go away. I wrote a

letter that day to Sir Edward Trafford, and asked the nurse to post it for me. She looked at the address critically.

'What are you writing to him for?' was her abrupt inquiry.

'My thanks.'

'Ah! well, it's right and proper you should be grateful,' she said; 'but he does not care for thanks, I know.'

I had not thanked him; I had only begged to see him for a few moments before I went away. I had implored him to honour me with a brief interview, to spare me from his golden minutes only one.

All that day and the next I lay resolving what I should say to him—what words that could show my gratitude, my sorrow, my remorse, without paining him too much. There was one confession which I wanted to make to him, one acknowledgment, but he did not come; and my orders were to go away, at last.

On the last day, when I was dressed and bidding good-bye to envious sufferers who had been near me, to nurses who had been kind to me, to young students and surgeons whose cheery words had brightened a few minutes of my sickness now and then, an attendant came up and said Sir Edward was waiting in his private room to see me before my departure.

My heart leaped with an unaccountable joy. He had relented, he had come to see me, he was waiting for me.

I went downstairs to the private room to which I was directed. I felt my heart beating quickly and painfully, my senses almost leaving me, as I stepped into the room and the door was closed behind me. He was sitting at a table writing, and he looked up keenly as I entered, and saw that I was strangely moved.

'You are not a strong man yet, Mr. Elwin,' he remarked very deliberately, 'and of any excitement you must be scrupulously careful. You should go down to the sea, and live a quiet, peaceful life, say for the next six months. I would recommend the Norfolk coast, or York-shire. Good-day.'

'No, Sir Edward, not good-day yet,' I replied promptly; 'I have something more to say, and I feel that I must say it to you. God brings me here to say it surely.'

'My time is not my own,' he answered, looking at his watch.

'Five minutes, sir. One minute, if you will allow me,' I pleaded.

'Take a seat. You must not try your strength too much, at present,' he said. 'I cannot afford you five minutes, I am afraid. Let us say three.'

'Very well.'

'Proceed, then. And pray be brief and cool.'

'In the first place, Sir Edward, let me thank you with all my heart for——'

'That would be wasting time,' he interrupted; 'I am here to do my duty, and need no thanks. I might thank you for the liberal donation which I hear you have given this morning to the funds of the institution; but being a wealthy man, that is your duty too— your gratitude.'

'Sir Edward,' I exclaimed, passionately, 'you

have saved my life. Tell me what to do with it,
in God's name.'

'And in God's name, sir, don't ask me,' was
his quick answer, and for an instant there was a
flame in his eyes I had not thought to see.

'It is *your* life. What shall I do with it
now?' I cried.

'I do not understand you,' he said, very coldly. 'Yours was a deeply interesting case, and
has afforded me an opportunity of testing a
theory of my own—of proving a fact that has
been long disputed by my contemporaries. I
was glad to find a subject—and there the matter
ends.'

'Not to me. It cannot end like this.'

'Pardon me, but it must. Three minutes!' he
said, looking at his watch.

'Sir Edward, I cannot go back to her,' I exclaimed; 'I cannot begin the life from which
my accident snatched me.'

'That is no business of mine.'

'I will make her independent of all worldly
cares, but I will not return to my old life. I
will not wrong you——'

'Pray do not rave of my wrongs, or of yours,' he said, with just the faint suspicion of mockery about his thin-cut lips. 'She did not break my heart when she was good enough to prefer you to me. I was the lucky man, not you. She was bad enough for me to despise and then forget, and there was an end of it. I cut the cancer away, and the scar does not give me pain.'

'Did you tell her I was in the hospital?'

'I told somebody to write—I forget whom—when we had discovered your address. She was asked not to come : an interview with you would have spoiled the best case that has ever come beneath my notice. And I was anxious to make a success of you. You are a success.'

'A success!' I groaned.

'To me, I mean.'

'To myself I am for ever a dead failure.'

He took up his pen again ; but, before he did so, he struck a bell at his side. The attendant appeared.

'Mr. Elwin is ready to go. Is his cab waiting?'

'Yes, Sir Edward.'

'May I say God bless you?' I asked. 'May I say, for all the past——'

'No; don't say any more, please. You worry me.'

'May I,' said I, approaching him, 'just touch your hand in love and gratitude—for once in all my misspent life, sir?'

There was a slight contraction of the massive brow, a shudder which he could not repress, and both his hands were put behind his back.

'No, no,' he said, quickly, 'not you! See him safely to the cab, Johnson—let him take your arm.'

But I had wrenched myself away from the attendant, and was stooping over him and whispering in his ear.

'As God is my judge,' I cried, 'I do not return to her. I cannot.'

'No. You cannot. That is quite impossible.'

'She—what do you mean?'

'She died in a lunatic asylum, a fortnight ago. A curious instance of mania about some children whom she had deserted ten years since.'

· Dead ! And I have not been told of this !' I exclaimed.

' It was of the greatest importance to keep the news from you,' said Sir Edward ; ' you would have spoiled my case. Take the gentleman's arm, Johnson again. Good morning.'

A BIG INVESTMENT.

A BIG INVESTMENT.

It is a goodish ten years ago since I was a junior partner in the firm of Flasher, Gudger, and Creech. I am Creech, a 'poor creech-ur,' Flasher used to say in his volatile moments, but Flasher thought himself a punster. Gudger considered Flasher 'a conceited hass,' and said so in confidence to me when business was not brisk. And I thought Flasher and Gudger, the couple of 'em, about as tricky and knowing a pair of mortals as I had ever met in the profession. But not a bad sort take them in the lump—far from it even.

I was intended for the law. My parents, respectable greengrocers in High Street, Peck-

ham, had determined that it should be the law,
when I decided for the circus, and ran away and
joined Poynder's troupe. I was fifteen when I
took to horsemanship in public ; in my private
capacity, and on my father's pony, I had already
distinguished myself to all my acquaintances as
a daring bare-backed steed rider. I was applaud-
ed by my contemporaries, and vaulting ambition
took me to Poynder's, where, though I say it
myself, I gathered fame by degrees, and earned
thirty shillings a week for years and years, more
years than I care to count now, mind you.

When Poynder's Circus came to grief, I had
put a little money by even out of my weekly
stipend of thirty shillings, and was enabled to
go into business on my own account. I took a
share in Flasher and Gudger's Museum of Wonders and World Renowned Emporium of Match-
less Marvels, and became the junior partner in
that show. Perhaps I was wrong, perhaps I
was not far out—I don't know. The advertise-
ment in the papers was very catching, and
Flasher and Gudger wanted capital. They
wanted novelty too, and they thought capital,

discreetly invested, would produce novelty. They had no capital themselves, save as it was represented by two boa-constrictors, a leopard that was always suffering from headache, two performing monkeys, a mechanical group of waxwork dolls representing Daniel in the lion's den, a two-headed child six inches long in a quart bottle of spirits of wine—the representation on the canvas was, I blush to own, that of a fat, double-headed youth in vigorous health, and in a bright blue suit of clothes—and the horse and caravan. The caravan wanted repairs, and the horse—Mayflower, aged seventeen, cocoanut kind of cataract on the left eye—was possessed of a constitution that was going rapidly to pieces for want of proper nourishment.

Still, I joined the firm. There seemed money in it, and I was too old to settle down. I was forty-five years of age then, and had been wandering about all my life, and I loved a wandering, hand to mouth, open air, vagabond's existence, as men and women do who drift early into it, and go here and there with the tide and never come to anchor. It's not a bad life. It's

not respectable, oh no! but oh! the lot of the
world you see, and the changes there are in it!
From bad to worse sometimes; but then there's
hard lines everywhere, even among you City
swells, as the penny papers tell us quick enough,
and when the hard lines come, you can't laugh
as we can at 'em—not you! You don't get
over 'em at the next town, or the next fair, or
in the next crowd at the sea-side. *We do.*

Well, they were not good times when I went
into partnership with Flasher and Gudger; but
I went into the concern with my eyes open. I
saw something might be done, and I paid thirty-
five pounds into the business and went in for my
· thirds,' and did my share of work with the rest
of them. I became the Chinese juggler and
fire-eater in professional hours. I was ' express-
ly imported from the interior of Chinese Tartary,'
and as I had juggled a good deal on horseback,
it was easy work on the floor of the Emporium,
and only wanted space.

With our curiosities living, dead, and bottled,
with myself for juggler, with Flasher for acting-
manager, comic vocalist, and Shakespearian

reciter, and with Gudger for a tattooed man, who had escaped by a miracle, and highly ornamented, from savages in the Caribbean seas—he was a sturdy, square man, whom we stencilled over with an elaborate pattern in indigo twice a week—we had not the worst show in the fair, take it altogether, and we jogged on. We did not make money; it was not money-taking times, and the two-headed prodigy caused no end of disputes for not coming up to sample outside, but Flasher was quick with his tongue, and could turn the laugh in his favour, pretty quickly too. He had been at it all his life, and knew what to say to put people in a good humour, and to thinking that their pennies had not been absolutely thrown away. Flasher had resources; Gudger had not. Flasher had a splendid imagination, allied to a reckless mendacity, and Gudger had no imagination at all. He was satirical at times, but anyone whose liver does not act properly is bound to be satirical. Gudger was a melancholy man, too, and full of forebodings. We were always going to the bad; it was always going to rain; the horse was always going to die ; we were never going to earn our salt, and when facts confuted his predictions he seemed rather sorry than otherwise, and was disposed to wish for bad luck next time to make up for it. But he was a hard working, honest soul after all, with a chronic hoarseness brought on by continual exposure of his tattooed torso to an agricultural or provincial public, and he had dreams of future greatness at times despite his moods of doleful prophecy.

'If we could only light on something new— something more of a novelty than pitching balls about and spinning daggers,' he said, with a half-contemptuous glance in my direction, ' we might make a little pile before we die—or get stone broke.'

' Quite right, old man,' said Flasher, always light and easy in his manner. ' We'll have a big investment some day. Trust me for that.'

' I hope we shall.'

' We've got talent; we're not moving, perhaps, with the times, but we're moving.'

' Oh, yes, we're moving ; if it's only to the

work'us, we're moving Joe,' remarked the ironical Gudger.

We were moving about Yorkshire then, making for Doncaster by slow degrees—very slow, because the horse was lamer than usual, and suffered from general debility, which not only necessitated the company's walking by the side of the show, but compelled a good deal of shoving the caravan behind whenever there was a little bit of hill-work. When we came to a decent village we had a 'pitch,' unrolled our canvases, and gathered in one or two stray pence, but the villagers were few and far between where it was possible to earn anything.

For three days I remember once we had not had a show; we had got a little out of our reckoning, too, and had lost ourselves in a dead and alive part of the country, where it was all hills and lumps of stone. Gudger was extra gloomy, and Flasher not in his usual spirits, when Mayflower suddenly came to a full stop, and gave up all efforts to proceed. It was a patient animal, but wise. It knew what it could do—what would happen to it if it over-exerted

s 2

itself, and it said, suddenly, and as plainly as if
it could speak, ' Gentlemen, this is very incon-
venient for the lot of us, I know, but I can't
move a step further, upon my honour. I give
up. I am done for the next twelve hours.
Urge me by brute force another hundred yards,
and I drop down dead as a door-nail, and not
sorry either to be out of such a hilly and rascally
world.'

We three tramps and ' diverting vagabonds'
sat by the roadside and stared hard at Mayflower.
We were all careful men and understood the
position at once. Showmen are acclimatised to
the unlooked-for. There was only the best to
make of it. We took Mayflower out of the
shafts, and Mayflower—very much like a gouty
man—hobbled slowly on to the moor, and then
lay down and tried to shiver itself to bits.
Flasher lighted his pipe ; and Gudger, who had
corns, crawled into the caravan and took his
boots off; I found some grass for Mayflower.

'What a beastly place to be wrecked in,'
said Gudger in a sepulchral voice from the
window.

'It's a bit breezy,' responded Flasher, 'but nice and fresh.'

'Fresh be hanged,' said Gudger. 'I can't keep a tooth still in my head.'

'Try a pipe?'

'Not on an empty stomach. Not me!'

'Then leave it alone.'

'I will.'

Flasher and Gudger had these spars occasionally when things went contrariwise, as they had done that day, but they soon got over their little differences. Half-an-hour's sulks, a faint burst or two of bad language, and it was all over. They had pulled together in harness too long not to understand each other's ways. They had their weaknesses of character; Flasher was of an over-sanguine temperament—a visionary; Gudger believed in the worst of everything, and was an excellent foil to the high flights of our senior partner; and I was the happy medium between the two.

After an hour or two Flasher and I went off in search of provisions; Gudger refused to lock up the caravan and accompany us. His corns

were 'orful bad, and he fancied Mayflower
might die before we came back. He did not
want anything to eat himself; he might be
going to die too, for what he knew; he felt
cussed queer all over, he said. Perhaps incess-
ant stencileing in indigo had struck at last into
his system.

When we were well ahead of the show, and
making for the top of the hill, I said—

'Gudger's getting worse and worse.'

'He's only put out a bit,' said Flasher; 'he'll
be as brisk as a bee to-morrow; brisker perhaps
—who knows?'

At the top of the hill we took a keen survey
of the country. It was too much country altogether. The whole thing was overdone.
Rough moorland broken by lumps of stone, and
backed by distant hills—a bleak, wild part of
Yorkshire, with not a cottage roof or sign of
chimney smoke showing up anywhere, even in
the far distance.

'This is a rum go,' said Flasher.

'I don't see what is to become of us.'

'There's a penny loaf on the top of the

monkey's cage that will do for us at a pinch, if
Gudger doesn't eat it before we get back, but
we want grub for the monkeys and a shin
bone for the leopard, and a lot of things.'

' Yes.'

' And we must step out till we find them,
that's all,' said the energetic Flasher.

And, by Jove, we did step out for miles and
miles, without meeting man, woman, or child,
and then we found we had overstepped the mark,
for, looking back to see if there was any sign
of the show, we saw, three-quarters of a mile in
the rear of us, in a dip of the land, and in what
looked like a disused quarry, a one-storied
cottage huddled in a corner out of the wind,
and with its one window, like a half-shut eye,
squinting at us from the distance.

' Come on, Ted,' said Flasher, ' there's land in
sight. Come on !'

Flasher had long legs, and the prospect of
refreshment and assistance gave an impetus to
them that quickly took him in advance of me.
When I reached the cottage I found him calmly
ensconced in a rush-bottomed chair, staring

with all his might and main at a very big, middle-aged, rosy-faced woman in a mob-cap, who sat in a capacious wooden chair by a small fire burning in the grate. A tremendous woman —the fattest female I had ever seen in my life.

She sat and smiled, nodded to me a welcome, and said 'Good day t'ye' in a broad Yorkshire accent that 1 will not scare my readers by trying to imitate in print. She looked the very picture of good-temper, and when Flasher remarked, 'This is my friend and partner,' she said in the most cheery manner, 'And I hope you're quite well, too, sir. Take a seat.'

I did so, and looked from the tenant of the cottage to Joseph Flasher as if for some kind of explanation. But Flasher continued to regard the lady with grave interest—I might say even with grave admiration.

'My good man will be back in a few minutes with the boys, and then he'll help you all he can, though he can't help you very much, I'm afeard,' said this cheerful and stout matron. 'You don't mind waiting?'

'Not a bit,' was Flasher's reply, 'we're tired and glad of a rest.'

'Ah! rest does a powerful sight o' good,' said the lady, 'though I have more than is good for me; sometimes I ain't hardly able to move for days.'

'I'm sorry to hear that,' said Flasher, politely. 'May I ask now what complaint?'

'It ain't a complaint; it's only weight. My mother was like it, so was my grandmother, I've heard.'

'You might have earned a lot o' money, the three of you,' said Flasher, regarding the position from a showman's point of view.

'I don't see it,' said the woman, with a chuckling laugh that was pleasant to hear, 'unless it was by sitting still. Oh, here's the good man and the boys. They know when it's dinner-time as well as most people, bless their hearts!'

There was a cloth spread for dinner, a huge dish of potatoes smoking in the centre of the festive board, and an uncut loaf of a very swarthy complexion at the side, and the preparation for the humble meal had evidently exhausted the strength of the lady of the house, who had been recovering from her exertion when my friend Flasher had arrived.

The good man and the boys—the man cadaverous and lanky, and in a torn smock frock, and the boys, five of them, ranging from seventeen to ten, in smock frocks too, that had been darned and patched in many places, and had possibly belonged to the father at an earlier period—looked very poor and hungry; there was an entire absence of that pleasant expression and amiable deportment which had surprised us in the fat woman. They all six glared at us in mute astonishment, and then stood round the table, clutched at the potatoes, and dabbed them into a plateful of salt, and ate voraciously, eyeing us distrustfully meanwhile. The woman joined them, and glanced apologetically towards us, as if she was sorry there was not enough to eat for the lot—which there was not, certainly. We were sorry for that too.

Presently, when the potatoes had disappeared, she explained the position, which Flasher had already made clear to her before I had arrived.

'Garge,' she said—she meant George, of course—'these gentlemen have had a breakdown on the road, and are obliged to stop till their horse is a bit better.'

Garge looked out of one eye at Flasher and me, and said, 'Oh!' and cut himself a slice of bread.

'They keep a show. Going on to Doncaster.'

Garge said 'Oh!' again, but was evidently not deeply impressed. The boys betrayed more interest, and regarded us attentively. The youngest went to the door and looked about him open-mouthed for the exhibition, returning with a sad expression.

'The gentlemen keeps wild beasts and sarpents and wants to get food for them, and are ready to pay for it, of course.'

'Oh!' said Garge again, whilst the boys betrayed renewed symptoms of restlessness and curiosity.

'I thought Farmer Shocks could help 'em a bit, Garge,' said the motherly female, and Garge said 'Oh!' for the fourth time, and thought it over quietly, or looked as if he was thinking it over.

'What's 'ee want?' he asked at last.

Flasher was the speaker, and detailed his requirements and what he expected to pay, and Mr. Oints—for that was the shepherd's name—thought over it for so long a time that we thought he had gone to sleep.

'Thee'd better go to old Shocks and talk to 'ee,' he said, suddenly.

'Will you show us the way?' said Flasher.

'It's my way,' said Mr. Oints.

'Oh, come on then.'

We were soon on the moor together making cross cuts for a farm that was evidently hiding about somewhere, and the lanky boys presently scattered and went their own ways, looking about them curiously for the show that had been talked of.

It was then that Flasher displayed his diplomacy by sidling closer to the sulky shepherd —for he was a bit sulky, or stupid—and saying,

'Your good lady is a wonderful woman, sir.'

'Won'erful fat,' was the reply.

'Might I ask, do you happen to know what her weight really is?'

'Noa, I don't.'

'With good living and plenty of nourishing things, she'd get bigger than that, Mr. Oints.'

'Then she won't get no bigger here,' said Mr. Oints, decisively.

'You mean you can't afford good living?'

'Never mind what I mean,' said Mr. Oints, 'she eats enuf, that's all.'

He did not seem to relish so much questioning, and turned his shoulder a little towards Mr. Flasher and hunched his back a bit. He was not an agreeable man, but Flasher drew him out at last.

'She'd be worth a couple of sovereigns a week to me,' said Flasher.

'What!' exclaimed Mr. Oints, roused suddenly to an intense interest in my partner's conversation; 'what's that you're talking about?'

Flasher repeated his assertion.

'D'ye mean a-showing her?' said Oints, with his little grey eyes ablaze now.

'That's what I do mean, old man,' was my partner's reply. 'It's a pity such a fine woman should hide herself away under a bushel.'

'What bushel?'

'Oh, bother,' interrupted Flasher, 'your wife would draw crowds to see her.'

'You should have seen her mother.'

'It's too late for that; never mind her mother, she'll do instead. If she'll come—if you'll take two quid a week, it's a bargain.'

'Two quid is two pounds?' asked the Yorkshireman.

'Yes, that's it.'

'Oh!'

He walked on in deep thought after this, and Flasher winked at me behind his back. I was excited, too, at the prospect of a new speculation which looked absolutely promising. We had made a discovery, we had found a prodigy, and Mr. Oints was very poor.

'You'll keep her in wittles—that won't be my look-out?' said Mr. Oints, suddenly.

' Oh, no.'

' She eats a lot when she can get it.'

' So she ought.'

' There'll be no drawbacks ?'

' Not a penny piece.'

' Where's the show ?'

Flasher told him, and he nodded his head slowly once or twice.

' I'll see you again,' he said.

And he saw us again later in the day, when Farmer Shocks had supplied us with all the necessaries of life for men and wild beasts, and we had found our way back to the show and to Gudger, who had eaten the penny loaf in despair, and whom we discovered fast asleep in a corner of the caravan. We found Mayflower better in health, but lame as a cat, and after feeding the animals and ourselves, we sat outside in the sun and talked of the money that was to be made by the exhibition of Mrs. Oints, until Gudger, who was a bit avaricious, began to be carried away by the eloquent description of Joe Flasher.

' She can't be as big as all that, Joe,' he said,

deprecatingly, and Joe took every oath he knew—and he knew a great many—that he was not exaggerating the ample charms of Mrs. Oints.

'Then the big investment has come,' said Gudger.

'She'll look a picture in white book muslin.'

'We must have a new painting outside,' I suggested.

'Leave it to me,' said Flasher.

'We shall make five pounds a week,' said Gudger.

'We shall make twenty,' cried Flasher, 'see if we don't.'

'But Oints won't agree, perhaps, or Mrs. Oints,' said Gudger. 'You've one fault, Joe— you're always so blooming cock-sure.'

'Ain't they all starving, Ted?' said Joe, appealing to me.

'Well, they ain't prospering.'

'Ain't he a miserly old hunks, who wouldn't offer a fellow a tater ?'

'Two fellers and two taters,' I corrected.

'Never mind. He wouldn't do it. And when

I said a couple of sovereigns a week, he lighted up like a bonfire.'

'He did.'

'Very well then. You wait and see.'

And we did wait. And just before it was dark he and his five sons came tramping down the road, the father to drive the best bargain with us that he could, and the sons to see the show for nothing.

To make a long story short, and to get to the more exciting part of this narrative, it may be said at once that the bargain was settled, even signed and sealed three days afterwards in the town of Doncaster itself, and a memorandum of agreement—for three years certain, with option of renewal for a similar period at an increased rate of wages—given to each party interested, and all legal formalities gone through and paid for out of the balance that was left from the purchase money of my share in the Emporium.

Mr. Oints had thought it over, and Mrs. Oints had thought it over, or had been talked over, and the good lady with the complacent manner, the large smile, and the appetite was duly con-

stituted one of the chief attractions of the
Emporium of Wonders, and was exhibited for
the first time at Doncaster with the most
tremendous success.

I can hardly tell you what a success it was,
or how we had pinched and struggled to make
it a success by expending every penny of our
substance in white book-muslin, and a new oil-
painting, and a printed poster in three colours.
Mrs. Oints was pleased, too, at her sudden
popularity, and her new book-muslin dress, and
with the comments of the crowd as to her pro-
portions, and if there were a happy family at
Doncaster, it was our noble selves. The tide
had turned and our heads were turned with it.

'We shall make thousands,' exclaimed the
sanguine Flasher.

'For gord's sake, Joe, don't let it be known
what we're taking,' said the cautious Gudger.

'Trust me.'

But Mrs. Oints was curious—Yorkshire folk
are just a little bit too curious, I fancy—and
wanted to know all about it.

'They're half orders,' said the mendacious

Flasher; 'must give away a lot of orders to begin with.'

'They come to see the tattooed man chiefly,' said Gudger, with a touch of conceit that was a little contemptible.

'Or the fire-king and prince of jugglers,' I added. 'At all events, it's the combination.'

'Ah! very likely,' said Mrs. Oints. with a heavy sigh that shook the show to its centre, for she was a woman who believed what was told her.

That sigh was startling; little did we think it was a forerunner of a variety of trials and troubles in store for us. We were elated with our success, but we were dancing on the brink of a precipice, and did not know it. People do indulge in that exercise sometimes in better circles of society than ours, I am told.

'I wonder what they are doing at Woolcombe,' she said, after the second day of the exhibition.

'What who's a-doing?' asked Gudger, who was dreadfully illiterate.

'Garge and the boys.'

T 2

'Can't say,' he added, unsympathetically.

'I've never been parted from Garge before,' she said.

'Haven't you, though?'

'Never.'

Then she heaved another sigh—and her sighs were as heavy as herself.

'Here, don't you go moaning and groaning all over the place,' said Gudger, who was quick to see the worst of everything; 'it ain't good for you.'

'Ain't it, sir?'

'No. It shakes the fat about,' he replied. 'It don't give it time to settle. You mustn't sigh like that.'

'I won't if you object to it; if I can help it.'

'You really must help it, my good woman.'

'Very well, sir. But I—I think I should feel happier if I could be sure Garge and the boys was a-getting on well without me.'

'Sure to be getting on well,' said Flasher, lightly, even flippantly, as he entered during this part of the conversation, 'why, there's more room in the place now.'

'More room doesn't mean more happiness, Mr. Flasher,' said Mrs. Oints, bursting into a flood of tears. And, when I say a flood, I mean a flood; I never saw a woman with so much cry in her.

'My good soul, for lor-a'-mussy's sake don't go on like this,' exclaimed Gudger. 'You mustn't fret, upon my soul you mustn't. You'll lose flesh, you'll bust up the whole concern. Do have a leetle consideration for other people, who've sunk a fortune in you.'

'I—I can't help it.'

'You'll have a letter from Oints in the morning.'

'He—he can't write.'

'He'll get somebody to write it for him,' said Flasher, 'and you'll read he's well and jolly, and got his two quid, and——'

'I—I can't read.'

'Well, I'll read it for you then,' said Joe.

'Thank you, sir.'

'Do you think a little rum and milk would bring you round a bit?' I suggested. I was always practical.

'Well, just a little sip, p'raps.'

We brought her a pint and a half, which she finished, and began to smile. The rest of the day she was comparatively cheerful. But Gudger (always Gudger) sowed the seeds of bitterness in the firm.

Later in the day he took Flasher and me aside.

'Blarm my eyes if she isn't getting thin,' he cried.

'Nonsense.'

''Taint nonsense,' said Gudger, indignantly. '*I* can see a difference in her.'

'Hasn't been time.'

'Yes, there has. Hers isn't solid, healthy fat, you may depend upon it,' said Gudger, 'it's a dissolving view almost.'

'Much you know about fat,' said Flasher, with a disparaging elevation of his nose.

But Gudger was right. The aggravating part of every dispute with Gudger was that he was generally right. A miserable and morbid mind, but too far-seeing for enjoyment of this world. Next day Mrs. Oints was weighed at a coal shed, to which we took her in the darkness of the night.

At the railway station, a week or so ago, she had bumped carelessly into the scales and dislocated the machinery, and there had been a violent altercation between Flasher and the railway porter—especially as Flasher had been weighing her surreptitiously—and Flasher had been delighted and booked the weight carefully at once. At the coal merchant's a change came over the spirit of our dreams. Mrs. Oints had lost eight pounds nine ounces, the weight of a decent leg of mutton.

'Cuss it,' said Flasher.

Later on in the night, when Mrs. Oints was sleeping in the caravan, and we were walking to our cheap lodgings in the town—an extra expense which had come to us since we had begun speculating in feminine marvels—Flasher said, suddenly and decisively,

'She mustn't get any thinner.'

'How are you going to help it?' said Gudger.

'We must keep her cheerful. We must stop

her fretting somehow, if we do it by violence. This mustn't go on,' he exclaimed, with excitement. 'And it shan't go on. Dashed if it shall.'

'Well?'

'She will have a letter from her husband to-morrow—a jolly letter, see if she doesn't,' he said, with a meaning nod.

And she did. Flasher arrived with it all fuss and bluster as usual, waving the missive over his head like a squib.

'Here you are, Mrs. Oints. A letter from Woolcombe at last,' he cried. 'I told you it wouldn't be long before you had one.'

'Oh, I'm so glad.'

'Thought you would be.'

'I've had such a sinking ever since daylight for fear I shouldn't hear from him.'

'Sinking, ma'am! Don't say a sinking.'

'But it was.'

'Did you ever try cod liver oil for sinkings?' he suggested.

'Never.'

'It's a capital remedy. I'll get you a pail

of it—a pint of it, I mean. You'll like it; you'll——'

'Where's the letter?' she exclaimed, not waiting for his further remarks.

Flasher tendered her the missive, which she turned over and over in her big hands critically.

'It didn't come by post,' she remarked at last.

'Yes, it did,' was Flasher's reply; 'it came enclosed in a letter to me acknowledging the receipt of the first two pounds. Shall I read it to you?'

'If you'll be so kind, Mr. Flasher.'

Flasher was only too ready to be kind. He opened the envelope, drew forth the letter, and began :

'"My dearest Matilda——"'

'What's that?' cried Mrs. Oints at once.

He repeated the term of endearment, and Mrs. Oints said, gravely,

'He never went on like that in all his life except at fair time, and many a year ago then. He's took to drinking—I'm sure he has. And,

oh, the poor boys ! what will become of them ?
—oh ! oh ! oh !'

'Hold hard, marm ! just hear what your good
gentleman has got to say before you flies off
again,' said Flasher ; 'I'm sure it's a cheerful
letter—a capital letter.   It looks like it.'

Flasher was quite right about the letter's
cheerful tone.   He had written every word of
it himself.

'Don't 'ee mind me, sir.   I'm a-listening,'
answered Mrs. Oints, drying her eyes.   'Please
go on ; and don't gabble quite so fast, please.'

Flasher read the letter.   In it, to begin with,
the fabulous Mr. Oints informed his wife that he
and her boys were as jolly and comfortable as
they could possibly be.

'They don't miss me a bit,' said Mrs. Oints,
with quivering lips ; 'la ! how soon a poor body
is forgot.   Just as if I was dead and gone and
put away a'ready.   And on'y a leetle week,
too !'

But they did miss her, it appeared.

' " We're uncommon jolly, but we miss you
very much, of course," ' Flasher went on, with

alacrity; ' " we can't sleep for thinking of you." '

'Can't sleep! Oh, poor dears. Oh, what will——'

' " Except in the night," ' added Flasher, impressively, ' " and then a clear and serene conscience gives us peaceful slumbers." '

' Gives 'em what?' inquired Mrs. Oints.

' Perfect rest. They go to sleep, you know. " The money which that good, kind fellow Flasher—to whom my respectful regards and compliments and eternal gratitude for taking care of you are due—has sent me conduces to the comfort and joy I feel; and you will be comfortable too, and free from all worrits, blessed with the conviction that you are doing your duty in that sphere of life to which it has pleased heaven to call you. Let us rejoice and keep up our spirits always in this time of universal prosperity, and

' " Believe me,

' " Your loving and ever faithful husband,
' " GEORGE OINTS." '

This was probably not a happy dash at the

style of the absent Mr. Oints, for the broad
countenance of Mrs. Oints shadowed at the
peroration.

'He must have been drinking awful hard
when he got somebody to say all that rubbish,'
she said, gloomily; 'and Garge can't stand
drink. I wonder who wrote it for him.'

'Farmer Shocks, I should say.'

'Farmer Shocks can't write either. Do you
think everybody goes about writing and reading
like a pack of children where I come from ?' she
cried, indignantly ; 'as if they hadn't something
better to do.'

'This old woman will be a trial to us,' said
Flasher, half an hour afterwards, as he wiped
the perspiration from his brow.

'She's a trial already,' said Gudger.

'We *must* keep her cheerful,' Flasher remarked. 'This is the aim and object of our lives.'

'We'll try.'

'Do you sing comic songs, Gudger ?'

'Never sang one in my life.'

'I can't do all the blessed work,' said
Flasher.

'Who asked you?'

'We must buy some comic books, and read them to her—some really laughable books—and amuse her that way after business. What's a good comic book, Creech?'

I had a literary bias, it was thought, and might help them with my advice in this matter, but I could only think of 'Captain Cook's Voyages' and 'Rasselas.'

'They won't do,' said Gudger, with withering contempt. 'We must take her to the play.'

And we did that very evening, and, as luck would have it, it was a lively piece, and kept her really amused and up to the mark till a fool of a flute-player squeaked out, 'Home, Sweet Home,' and then we had to hustle her out of the premises in violent hysterics.

The next day there came a letter from the veritable Mr. Oints to his wife—a spludgy epistle, with the spelling abominable and all downhill. Flasher—never too particular a fellow—felt that he could not show such a letter as that to Mrs. Oints, so he opened it and read

it aloud to Gudger and me before putting it in
his pocket out of the way.

There was no 'Dearest Matilda,' no amiable
prefix to the letter at all, in fact. It went at
once to business and startled us.

'"You mustn't think of kummin' back,"' it
began, ' "so it's no use sending no more
letters.'"

'She's got somebody to write for her,' ejaculated Flasher.

'Who is the traitor?' asked Gudger, looking
at me, 'who is the worm in the bud that turns
agin us?'

'It ain't him, so shut up,' said Flasher.
'"Don't let that old woman write any more,
becos I don't want to 'ear."'

'It's Mother Warts,' said Gudger.

Mrs. Warts was an estimable and venerable
lady whom we had discovered in Doncaster
willing to tidy up and char the caravan twice a
week for four shillings and her food and two
orders for admittance to her nephews.

'Warts or no Warts, it matters not,' said
Flasher, loftily; then he read on, '"It's in the

contract you're to stop, and stop you will. So
no more at present, from Garge Oints." '

'An unfeeling, mercenary brute, sirs,' said
Flasher. 'We will spare his wife such an
epistle as this. I will write her a much better
one before the week is out.'

'Is this quite on the square?' I ventured to
inquire.

'Perfectly,' said Flasher, airily, 'self-pre-
servation is the first law of nature, and Mrs.
Oints cannot afford to lose another ounce.'

But she did lose a quantity of ounces. She
had recklessly thrown away six more pounds
when we weighed her with great care the
following week. And yet we did work hard to
amuse her. We exerted ourselves to the utmost.
We were ingenious in subtle devices to bring a
smile to her countenance. Gudger tried hard
to be comic even, and made such ugly faces
over his anecdotes—acting his stories, he called
it—that Mrs. Oints thought his brain was soften-
ing, and refused to be left alone with him.
Flasher thought conundrums might relieve her
mind, but they only harassed and perplexed her.

She never guessed one, and she did not appear
to understand when they were explained to her,
and the practical jokes he played on me—which
we planned between us sometimes—only re-
minded her of her louts of boys on Sundays,
and brought copious tears into her eyes again.
A settled gloom fell upon Gudger and me, even
a shade of carking care finally flitted across the
genial countenance of Flasher.

'If this goes on we shall be ruined,' said
Gudger.

'She's big enough at present; she can afford
to lose a stone or two,' said Flasher, 'but I
don't like it.'

'I should think you didn't.'

'After the races she shall have some sea air,'
said Flasher; 'it'll give her tone.'

'She don't want no tone; she eats like a
horse.'

'*That's* a good sign,' said Flasher.

But it was not a good sign with Mrs. Oints.
The appetite increased, but her form decreased.
She became resigned—I think the dinners tended
to resignation, perhaps—but peace of mind did

not produce any further development of body. On the contrary, week after week showed a serious deficit, and sea-air made her nearly thin. We tried Blackpool, as it was bracing; we toiled and worked through Lancashire to get to Blackpool, and then the place was out of season, and the wind blowing the roofs off the houses, and the shops half shut, and the streets very nearly empty. We had a row at Blackpool, too. One man said Mrs. Oints was no bigger than his mother, and wanted his money back, and this eventually led to blows between him and Flasher, and to Flasher having two black eyes.

The Fates were really against us. The big investment was not likely to turn out well. It was our luck.

'I know what I'd do with Mrs. Oints,' said Gudger, one day very gloomily after sitting for an hour on the caravan steps, with his face buried in his hands.

'What would you do?' inquired Flasher, a little unceremoniously; 'it's something for you to have an idea; out with it, Gudger, before it escapes you.'

'I shouldn't give her any more food,' said Gudger.

'What!'

'It's a waste,' he continued.

'Our only chance,' said I, 'is to keep her up.'

'We'd better keep her down,' continued Gudger. 'She's disposed to go down, ain't she, and presently we can exhibit her as the *Living Skeleton*, and get our money back that way,' said the miserable man.

'Gudger,' said the senior partner, 'I'm astonished at you. I'm shocked. I mean it. It's irreverence. It's flying in the face of—we'll take her to the doctor's this afternoon,' said Flasher, 'and see what he can do.'

We took her to the doctor, who congratulated her on getting rid of so much superfluous flesh, and prophesied that it would be much better for her health. He had no more consideration for the results of our speculation than a pig. He would not look at it from that point of view for a moment. He would not understand that fat was her normal state, and that when she was getting thin she was becoming unnatural in the highest degree.

We wrote to Oints a touching letter at last —this was when Mrs. Oints was resigned to us, and not a bit bigger than any other woman—and informed him that she was grieving dreadfully for home, that the doctor thought she had a compound complication of Nostalgia (we found that name in the dictionary), and that we would not answer for the consequences if she were not taken back at once.

Oints's solicitor replied promptly and sharply, and referred us to the memorandum of agreement. He also asked to see a medical certificate from a duly qualified practitioner as to Mrs. Oints's present condition, and Flasher immediately proceeded to write one, till I told him that that kind of game might lead to penal servitude, when he said he would think it over a bit more, which he did, and gave up the idea.

Still, it must be recorded to the credit of Flasher, Gudger, and Creech that they kept to their agreement as long as the show's receipts would allow of two pounds a week to be settled on the mercenary Oints, who kept an eye upon us, and seemed to always know, though he never stirred from Woolcombe, whereabouts at the end of the week we were likely to be situated. He had a bad habit at last of sending some one for his money every Saturday, as though he doubted us.

Perhaps this was the last feather; perhaps it was the death of the leopard with brain fever— his head had not ached for nothing all these years—perhaps it was the extra resignation to her surroundings that Mrs. Oints suddenly evinced; but one early morning when we were outside York, and the incubus seemed to us within easy and comfortable distance of home, to be passed on by one or two friendly parishes if she got short of funds, we made up our minds to fly the whole concern—to fly the country, if it was necessary.

We were in debt to an agent, and there was an embargo on the show, the two boa-constrictors. the monkeys, the boy in the bottle, the caravan, and Mayflower. Also on the leopard, our most valuable asset, which had gone to

a better world where leopards are at peace—
and we knew the information of the animal's
• decease would bring on the foreclosing of the
loan from Isaac Moss, of Liverpool.

It is a sad confession as a wind-up to this
story—it leaves it utterly without a moral—but
we shook hands sadly with each other one
wintry evening, and went our separate ways,
and were never heard of more. That is, under
our own names. What became of Gudger is a
mystery to this day—some one thought he had
seen him preaching at the corner of a street, but
he could not say for certain. Flasher fell on his
feet and became a chairman at a music hall, and
wore a dress suit, and studs you could not tell
from diamonds, and his easy ways made him a
great favourite. I went back to circus life, but
it was only to groom horses and hold horses for
other people Ah, well ! such a life.

What became of Mrs. Oints we never knew.
I cannot say that we ever cared much, she had
embittered the last days of the Emporium so
terribly.

'Perhaps she is still sitting in the caravan in

white book-muslin waiting for us to come back, Joe,' I said one evening, when Joe Flasher was standing me a drink at the bar of the Electric . Spark Music Hall in Houndsditch.

'Let her wait,' said Joe, vindictively.

He had got on in the world at least, but he had not forgiven Mrs. Oints.

There are some wrongs which a man never forgives: being done out of his money is, perhaps, the cruelest wrong of all.

THE STONE BOUQUET.

THE STONE BOUQUET.

CHAPTER I.

EVERYBODY said it was not likely to turn out well—but then everybody is so wise. And what everybody says must be true, especially when it is upon a subject which nobody understands and nobody takes to heart, but the one poor biped who is principally concerned. Was everybody right in my case—and was I so egregiously wrong? So blind, so shallow, so vain? He who reads these lines shall judge for himself. I have lost the faculty of judging; I am waiting for a greater judgment, and wondering what it will be like. Whether I shall be

able to plead my own extenuating circumstances—the fact that I was always true and
earnest, and that I loved her with my whole
heart, and would have died for her at any moment. And that, in loving her so much, I
wrecked at last the little sense which I had ever
had.

I married Cicely Grey when I was forty years
of age, and she was a girl of nineteen. An ill-
matched pair, an ill-assorted couple, the beginning of the old story, May and December
almost: the impulse of youth on one side, the
glamour of the ‘well-off man’ on the other.
That is what the world said. My petty little
world! Yes, I *was* well-to-do. That is, I had
attained a certain position in my profession, had
made my mark as an engineer, had been successful in one or two important schemes, was
spoken of—a little—at home and abroad as a
clever and rising man. Almost a genius.

I had studied hard all my life, it was asserted.
I had sacrificed everything to the pursuit of
fame, or of money. I was a close, keen man of
business, and had let nothing stand between me

and my profession. I was thorough. And then
Cicely Grey stood between—took me into another world, changed the whole current of my
life, made of me a passionate lover in my
middle age. That fate befalls a man at times
when he loves not in his youth—'Wait till he
comes to forty years,' and a man will laugh
at love, proclaims the great cynic. But the
cynic is not always right, and that man who
is an exception to the rule—well, woe betide
him!

I met Cicely Grey, and loved her—loved her
all the more passionately because I had not had
the time to love before—had laughed at the
romance of youth from the grim seclusion of
my study wherein I had immured my better self.
When the time came—when I was almost famous—when people pointed me out as Haviland
the engineer, I found that I could love as deeply as other men, and be as great a fool in my
own way. And with my youth gone, and when
flecks of white were in my hair, I knew this, and
hoped and prayed one fair young flower would
turn to me too, and take me to her heart, and

think the best of me—think me the best of all
the men whom she had ever known!

She was not then twenty years of age,—' old
enough to be my daughter,' people said, of
course. They always say that. And *that* was
terribly near the truth. But I was not *quite*
like other men, and this was my first love. I
had had none other. It was a new life to me.
Cicely Grey had been brought up in seclusion;
she was the daughter of one of my own craft—
an engineer who had been knighted by his
sovereign. She knew as little of the world—
the hard, real, artificial world—as I did, I was
sure. Men are so sure of what they wish. The
pieces of the puzzle—a fair-woman puzzle—fit
in so well to the wish of the egoist. He sees
no faults, and is deaf to the whispers of the
crowd. He is a blind man in his adulation. It
is as well, sometimes; but often, alas, it is not
always well.

Cicely had been left motherless at an early
age, and girls who have grown up to woman-
hood without their mothers are to themselves
and to other folk three parts a mystery. They

have lost so much. The life about them is without the white light to show the way and train the faltering footsteps. They are not always to blame, these motherless girls. Was Cicely Grey to blame for marrying me, for not telling all the truth, for disguising from me the one romance of her life in which no one had shared but the man who was the hero of it? The man of whose existence I had not dreamed, and whose name had not passed her lips? Was her father to blame, who had some hazy notions of the truth and of the misery of a *mésalliance*, and had trusted to time, and travel, and *me*—his old friend—to sink a past folly wholly out of her remembrance? I cannot say. In later days it was intimated to me that the father had left it to the daughter to explain, to laugh away if she could with a few careless words, about a school-girl's fancy that had flourished and died away, and so an end of it; and the daughter had thought the father might tell me and leave me to consider the position, and hence between the two the silence, and the ignorance—which was bliss then.

It would have been all the same had the story
been told me word for word; it would not have
swerved me aside—from her—by one hair's
breadth; it would have been no grievance *then*.
I could have laughed with the father, sympa-
thised with the daughter, and passed the whole
thing by. Later on 1 did not laugh, but sat
down before an awful truth and let it kill me
by degrees.

We were married in the early summer, and
went away for a long tour through the most
picturesque portion of our native land. We
eschewed foreign travel: we had had enough of
the continent, we both thought; business had
taken me abroad very frequently, and Cicely
had been educated in Paris and knew but little
of England. She would not care to go abroad
for her honeymoon, she said.

It was a honeymoon that presaged much of
happiness for us both—all was so fair: life had
changed for both of us so much, and all about
our new world was fresh and bright.

After our marriage in town we started from
the church doors for the country. I had wished

to evade all the fuss and frivolity of a wedding-party; I had felt that I should be looking too old and lined and grey at a marriage-feast, and that the guests would whisper of 'sacrifice' and 'monetary considerations' and 'poor girl' to each other, whilst wishing us every happiness. Cicely had not demurred; my will was hers, she said.

'I shall be always very obedient, Ulric,' she said to me, laughing, 'and my clever old husband will always have his own way.'

I laughed too, but the word 'old' jarred a little. It was not pleasant for me to consider myself old, or getting old, yet awhile, when I was beginning my real life. It was more unpleasant still that she should think so, even in jest. And I was so young at heart. Good God, how young I was then—what a little I knew of woman or a woman's ways—altogether, what a fool!

There was sight-seeing in the little town into which we first took refuge. Though we had not bargained for it or thought of it, it was a show place in its way. I will call it Heather-

combe, for a reason that I have. Here we were
to spend a quiet, halcyon week, surrounded by
all the beauties of hill and dale, of forest and
fell, and intensely restful in our own society.

' I am sure I shall be very happy all my life,'
she had confessed to me, ' for I know how well
I can trust you.'

She had put her hands into mine in saying this,
and looked at me unflinchingly and with all the
clear depths which her great grey lucid eyes
could express.

The emphasis struck me even then.

' Have you ever trusted in vain?' I asked,
laughingly. For it did not seem possible that
one could do anything to deceive her by word
or deed,

' I have been too imaginative, that is all,' she
answered, ' too sanguine, impulsive, hopeful.'

' Good faults, one might call them all.'

' I have expected too much—set my friends
on too high pedestals,' she said; ' young people
always do.'

' And some of the idols have been top-heavy
and tilted over,' was my rejoinder. ' Ah! never

mind, child ; they were not worth the trouble of
putting back in their places.'

'They were not,' she said.

We were wandering in the gardens of this
little town. It was our wedding eve. I have
said Heathercombe was to a certain extent a
show place, and in these gardens was one of the
wonders of the county. It boasted a rocky
mound over which trickled and spluttered a
stream of water with properties of turning into
stone anything exposed to its action for a certain period of months. Such wells are not uncommon in England or abroad, I believe ; but it
was a novelty to both of us, and there was
pleasant jesting over it, and over the various
articles which the preceding sight-seers had left
to be petrified—gloves, feathers, hats, and all
kinds of odd tokens, suspended in such a manner from the rock as to bring them in contact
with the stream.

'I know !' cried Cicely, clapping her hands.
'Wait for me, Ulric, I shall not be a minute.'

But a minute out of sight then was an hour
of suspense to a love-sick man. Where can

she have gone, what can have happened, I was
wondering five minutes afterwards. Yes, she
was impulsive at all events, and full of strange,
odd conceits. Presently she returned from the
hotel with her wedding bouquet that she had
brought from London—that I had sent to her
early that morning—a poem in fair white blos-
soms from a Covent Garden florist.

'This shall not wither away, Ulric, but be
always with us—a memento, a record.'

'Love turned to stone,' I answered, a little
ruefully ; 'is it a good idea ?'

'Yes ; a proof of love that endures,' she said.
'That is what I mean.'

It was a strange conceit, but I had no objec-
tion to urge. Let it be so. There was poetry
in the fancy, looking at it in the right way.
Love perpetual and that nothing should wither !
So the bouquet was left with the custodian of
the dripping well, and no more was thought of
it for awhile.

That is the prologue to my story.

CHAPTER II.

THEY were twelve months of happiness which
followed. Even the sceptics only muttered
'How long will it last, we wonder?' There
was not a cloud in our heaven; I studied every
wish, and she was grateful for it. At times
there came a faint, far-away doubt if she were
as happy as myself—might be only happy in
the second degree, taking her life and lightness
from me—content and at peace, seeing that I
was content, but not the life and light natural
to her own young self. A passing doubt even
this, and which she laughed away when I
expressed it once, in the grave earnest fashion
that was common to me, that would make me
look stern and thoughtful at times, even when
my heart was too full of joy for words.

There came no child to hallow our union, and we both regretted it. There was never a child to complete the links in the home chain ; surely it would have been so different had it been God's will to bless us thus. I think I see this now ; I feel it more acutely every day between this and the end of it. And yet if all *had* happened the same, what an extra torture for the child—what a heritage of horror when it became impossible to hide the truth, that truth, which some snake would have hissed out somewhere.

A little more than twelve months after this I was compelled to leave England again. The opportunity was too great and grand for a man of my profession to miss ; it was the talk of the world at that time, and I was congratulated on my good fortune at every turn. But my mission for some three years lay in a far-away wild quarter of the world, where a woman's health, perhaps her life, would be necessarily in jeopardy. There was rough work, if great work, even for men ; so I was to go my way alone for awhile, and it was arranged that Cicely was to return to her father's home and keep house for him, as in the old days, till I came back again.

The last night I spent in England was at a ball given by an aristocratic friend. I had not intended that it should be spent in this fashion. I had thought there was a clear week longer for me at home, when a telegram arrived urging the necessity of my immediate departure.

Cicely turned pale.

' It is to take you away from me,' she said.

' Yes.'

' When ?' was the next eager inquiry.

' To-morrow.'

' Then we will not go to this ball. I do not want to dance on the brink of my desolation,' she cried, bursting into tears.

Till that hour she had been very brave, very sure that it was all for the best, for my fame's sake and name's sake, but this sudden cutting away time from under her feet unnerved her.

' Cicely, if you wish me to stop—if—' I said.

' No, Ulric, you must go,' was her reply, ' don't mind me. I am only surprised. Our

parting is not for all time—you will be back
again soon. I shall not be so very old, so very
much changed when you return to me.'

We did not break our engagement to the
dance. Dancing was her passion, and I was
pleased in watching her pleasures, and content
with a quiet quadrille or two for my share in
the festivities. I thought the evening's excitement would distract her thoughts from the grim
fact of our premature separation, and that in
the morning, when she was tired out and resting
peacefully, I might be able to steal away without the ordeal of a bitter parting, sparing her
and myself some pain. I was afraid she would
break down utterly in a last leave-taking, and
that the remembrance of her sorrow would un-
nerve me, perhaps bring me back to her before
my task was done.

It was a great ball in its way—that is, there
were many guests, and the rooms were crowded
with men and women of rank and distinction.
After our first dance together, Cicely was lost
to me amidst a host of partners, and I was left
to discuss commonplaces with middle-aged

contemporaries, to receive various congratula-
tions on my appointment, to talk right and left
of the very subject which I was trying hard to
avoid.

Presently I found myself watching Cicely
from the door of the ball-room; my eyes had
wandered in search of her for some time in vain,
and then I found her sitting in the recess of a
window, whose heavy curtains almost concealed
her from view. It was only by the fan, a large
and heavy fan of ostrich feathers quaintly
grouped together, that I knew it was she. She
was sitting with her back towards me, half
hidden in the recess—it was only a half-outline
of her graceful figure that I saw there, but I
was sure it was Cicely.

That was the first heart-stab which I had
ever had. On that night there seemed to open
out to me by slow and sure degrees the consciousness that I might not have won the love
of my wife so wholly and completely as. to
render us safe together or apart. My trust in
her, my own self-esteem, had received no shock
till that hour, but here was struck the first

jarring note of a whole soul's discord. I woke
as from a dream, and I was none the better for
the waking. There came even then to me the
consciousness that I might be a very Othello in
my jealousy, if God so willed that an angel
should prove false. I did not know till then
that I was an intensely jealous man: she had
been so fair and fond a wife, she had cared so
little for the admiration of other men, and had
even taken pains to evade it. It was not from
my wife's manner that this jealousy suddenly
obscured my reasoning powers, my keen fore-
sight, my knowledge of human nature, every
gift with which other people had credited me.
My suspicion came from the man with whom
she was conversing. I could see him plainly
from my post of observation—a tall, dark man
of three or four and twenty years of age, with a
handsome and impassioned face, and black
eyes which seemed to flash like diamonds with
the torrent of words which he was pouring forth
to her.

It was the life in that face, its earnestness, its
rapt expression, its forgetfulness even of the

scene in which he formed a part, the gestures
which betokened the absorbing nature of his
conversation. Of what could he be talking to
Cicely, to betray so much excitement and
earnestness, what theme of such deep moment
to them both to give that strange look to him?

My heart sank like a plummet in the sea. I
was aware of danger to me, to Cicely—I hated
him already. I felt this was no common man
standing between me and the happiness of my
life; the power in him to influence that life for
good or evil was apparent to me at once—I
knew it by some subtle instinct. by the sudden
warning which came to me from heaven—or
hell—as no warning ever came before. A
friendly hand fell upon my shoulder, and startled
me. It was my host, Lord Sandbourne, who
stood laughing at my surprise.

'What, dreaming, Haviland?' he said.

'A reverie, my lord—a summer-night's dream
of going away and leaving all this bright life to
others.'

'Gad, I wish I could go with you. I should
be glad.'

Lord Sandbourne had had a craze for out-of-
the-way expeditions, and had wandered over
half the world in his day, and written many
wearisome books that nobody cared to read.

I did not continue the subject.

' Who is the good-looking young fellow talking to my wife ?' I asked, very lightly—too
lightly to be natural—but Lord Sandbourne was
not critical.   He put up his eyeglass and stared
in my direction.

· Gad, I don't know ; I never saw him before,'
he said.   ' Lady Sandbourne sows her invitations
broadcast, and I leave the crop to her.   This
sort of thing is woman's business, you see.'

' Yes, I suppose so.'

I walked away from him.   I made my way
quietly and almost steadily towards the recess.
I felt like a man playing the spy.   I was not
in any way like Ulric Haviland that night.   I
was a new man who had begun a new life.
A dark life, with the light of the old one dying
out, though I would not have believed it then for
all the world, although five minutes afterwards
there did not seem much doubt of it to me.

When I was close to them, the truth was close too. Neither had heard me approach; the whirl of the dancers past. the braying of a waltz from the orchestra, the place in which they were seemed security itself, and these two did not take heed of me, in their self-absorption.

'Why did you marry then? Why could you not wait and believe in me?' were the words which this indiscreet raver uttered to my wife, who was shrinking back from him, and trembling and flushing. whose eyes were swimming in hot tears.

'Cicely,' I said, with suppressed coolness, as I stood before them, 'I have been wondering what has become of you.'

My wife rose and put her hand on my arm.

'I am glad you have come, Ulric : I have been waiting for you,' she exclaimed. 'Take me home. I am tired of all this,' she added, speaking very rapidly.

'Who is this gentleman?' I asked, in a low voice.

'Madame Haviland will introduce me to her husband,' said the man before me, in a foreign

accent; and Cicely said, still hurriedly and like
a woman under a spell,

'This is my old friend, Monsieur Danano,
whom I knew once in Paris.'

' Oh, indeed.'

· Monsieur Danano—now of the French opera
—of whom you have probably heard, Ulric.'

The name was not unknown to me.

' Yes, I have heard of Monsieur Danano.'

' As I, sir, have heard of the name of Mr.
Haviland, the famous engineer,' he said, with a
low bow, and a smile which I did not return.
He had recovered from the surprise of my ap-
pearance, the excitement of his own avowal;
whether I had heard any part of his conversation to my wife or not, did not appear to
matter to him. With perfect ease and self-
confidence he said,

'You have probably been familiar with my
name, Mr. Haviland, before the Parisian world
thought it worth mentioning above a whisper.'

' No, sir.'

' I was an old friend of madame's—almost an
old schoolfellow—very nearly what you English

call "an old flame." I was saying,' he added, as he looked keenly and yet laughingly at us both, 'when you did me the honour to arrive, that Madame Haviland might have waited a little longer for me. But I am vanquished,'— here he bowed again—'and you, sir, are the victor.'

One could but try to smile at this bold, but good-humoured explanation, and then with a light word or two I bore my wife away from him. She was anxious to get home, she said, and I took her at her word. Why should I doubt it yet?

END OF THE SECOND VOLUME.

LONDON : PRINTED BY DUNCAN MACDONALD, BLENHEIM HOUSE.

www.ingramcontent.com/pod-product-compliance
Lightning Source LLC
Chambersburg PA
CBHW020808060726

47498CB00017B/1089